She was afraid of betraying her feelings

She felt his free hand touch her shoulder, cupping it firmly, his fingers warm against her skin, and she jumped as if stabbed. Pulling away from him, she turned her head just in time to see his face settle into a mask of hard withdrawal.

"I'm sorry," Callum said distantly.

For what, Rosy wanted to ask. *For showing me just what the physical relationship between man and woman can be...for showing me what love can be?* She wanted to tell him that she was the one who was sorry. But she didn't trust her voice, so she shook her head instead.

"I take it that yesterday is something you want to forget," Callum said tersely.

Forget? Never. But for his sake....

FRANCES RODING is fast becoming a popular name in romance fiction. The author lives in England and has enough story ideas to make writing a lifelong career.

Books by Frances Roding

FRANCES RODING

---

gentle deception

Harlequin Books

TORONTO • NEW YORK • LONDON
AMSTERDAM • PARIS • SYDNEY • HAMBURG
STOCKHOLM • ATHENS • TOKYO • MILAN

Harlequin Presents first edition August 1990
ISBN 0-373-11293-9

Original hardcover edition published in 1989
by Mills & Boon Limited

CHAPTER ONE

'WILLIAM! Quick, in here!' Miranda Bellaire hissed to her youngest brother. She was standing in the half-open doorway to her bedroom, glancing up and down the very pretty landing of their eldest sister's home with an expression of purposefulness which William recognised with suspicion.

'What's wrong now?' he demanded in unfriendly tones as she half pulled him inside the room, not giving him the opportunity to escape. 'And if you want to borrow some money from me you're out of luck...'

'Borrow money—off *you*!' Mirry said scornfully. 'I'll have you know, I don't need to borrow money off anyone. *I'm* the owner of a very promising design business and...'

'And would be sitting in some sweat-shop somewhere sewing clothes for someone else if Elliott hadn't staked you,' William told her ruthlessly.

'All right.' She tossed her head disdainfully. 'And *you* wouldn't be at Oxford if Elliott wasn't financing *you*.' Mirry retaliated with fraternal brutality, and then remembered why she had wanted to speak to him in the first place, and abandoned the argument, saying instead, 'William, we've *got* to do something about Rosy.'

'What do you mean?' William asked her uneasily.

'Isn't it obvious? Ever since she came down here and started working for Elliott, Bea has looked so miserable.'

'How do *you* know that? You've only been here for the last week, and Rosy arrived over a month ago. Anyway, Bea likes her. It was Bea who invited her to stay.'

'Yes, but that was before...'

'Before what?' William asked, mystified, becoming impatient with his sister and her rambling conversation.

'Before Elliott and Rosy started spending so much time alone together,' Mirry said importantly.

William stared at her. 'But Rosy's helping Elliott with his charity work,' he protested.

Mirry made a sound of deep disgust at this pragmatic statement and said ruefully, 'Rosy is falling in love with Elliott. And now that Bea's having another baby...'

'Twins,' William reminded her gloomily. 'I'm going to be an uncle to twins.'

'Yes. Well, that makes it even more important that we get rid of Rosy, doesn't it?' Mirry interrupted him. 'Just imagine poor Bea left on her own with four children!'

William wasn't imagining any such thing. He was far more concerned by the ominous portent of Mirry's suggestion.

'What exactly do you mean, get rid of her?' he asked cautiously, all too aware of his sister's impulsive schemes.

'We need to get her away from this house and Elliott. I suppose it's only natural that she should be tempted to fall for Elliott,' Mirry allowed large-mindedly. 'He *is* very attractive in a sort of primitively male way, I suppose,' she mused, ignoring William's derisive snort. 'And, of course, to have found out that you have a second cousin like Elliott after believing that you have no family at all... As far as Elliott's concerned...well, she *is* very attractive...'

'And Bea isn't?' William suggested mildly, the blue eyes behind his glasses sparkling militantly at Mirry's suggestion that his favourite sister was not just as attractive as her husband's newly discovered second cousin.

'Well, of course she is, but Rosy...well, Bea doesn't get a lot of time to spend with Elliott these days, does she, what with the children and now being pregnant again? And now that Rosy is living here in the house... You must see the danger.'

'Not really,' William told her unhelpfully. 'In fact, I think the only danger to Bea's marriage is inside your head, and if you think I'm going to let you involve me in one of your crack-brained schemes...'

'My schemes are *not* crack-brained,' Mirry protested, her voice rising in indignation. 'Oh, you're useless, William. If only Seb or Ben were here.'

'Well, they're not,' William told her flatly, scowling a little at the mention of their older twin brothers, one of whom was in Hollywood working on a new film and the other starring in a Broadway production of a British play. 'And if you honestly think that Rosy's the type to try to break up Elliott and Bea's marriage...'

'Oh, I didn't say she would deliberately set out to do something like that,' Mirry put in hastily. 'It's just that the temptation must be there. Oh, come on, William,' she wheedled. 'It wasn't as though I was going to ask you to do anything particularly difficult ... just invite Rosy to partner you to a few of those parties and dinners they're always having at Oxford ... Introduce her to some of your friends ... Some of your tutors ...' she added thoughtfully. 'Bea was saying she met the most fabulously charismatic——'

'George Lansdowne,' William interrupted her flatly. 'Gorgeous George, wc call him. He has women standing in queues three-deep,' he added in disgust. 'Anyway, he's on a lecture tour in the States at the moment.'

'Well, there must be others,' Mirry interrupted hastily. 'I bet Oxford is just bursting at the seams with available men who'd love to be introduced to a beautiful blonde like Rosy.'

'Forget it,' William told her rudely. 'There's nothing wrong with Rosy's relationship with Elliott. She's grateful to him, that's all ... and to Bea.'

'Oh! Oh, brothers ...' Mirry yelled, hurling a pillow at him as he opened the door and dodged past it.

Trust Mirry to get some bee in her bonnet about Rosy and Elliott, William reflected wryly as he went downstairs. He supposed that was *her* legacy from their parents: her far too active imagination.

He personally could barely remember either of their famous parents. Both of them had been at the height of their acting careers when they had been killed, and he, their youngest child, had only very dim memories of them. Bea had brought him up, and after what he had heard of his parents from his older siblings he was more than grateful for that fact.

On the way past Elliott's study, he paused outside the half-open door, hearing voices inside, Elliott's clear and decisive, holding an amused thread of warmth, and then Rosy's, soft and feminine as she made some response. He hesitated on the point of going in, conscious of an intimacy between the two people in the room that made him uneasily recall Mirry's warning. Rosy and Elliott—ridiculous—or was it? Always fiercely protective of his eldest sister, he suddenly realised how little any of them actually knew about Rosy. And, as Mirry had pointed out, Elliott was a very attractive man, and Bea was tied down with two small children and another pair on the way. The door was half-open, but neither of them had seen him. Normally ungainly and clumsy in his movements, he managed to back away from the door without betraying his presence. He fumbled with his glasses, a habit he had when something upset him.

Listening to Mirry, he had not for one moment believed a word of what she was saying. Bea and Elliott's marriage was as steady as a rock ... or so he had believed. Now, suddenly, he was not so sure.

He had reached the kitchen door without re-alising it. It opened as he approached it, and Bea herself came through. She looked rather pale and tired, and he felt a savage rush of anger against his brother-in-law. Two children both under five and now two more on the way... Couldn't Elliott *see* how exhausted Bea looked... or didn't he care any more?

'William...what's wrong?'

He gave her a guilty look and flushed darkly. He had never been any good at hiding his feelings from Bea.

'Nothing.'

'Mm...quarrelled with Mirry again, have you? Is Elliott in his study? I want to have a word with him.'

'No, don't go in there...'

In his agitation, William caught hold of her arm, and then released it almost immediately, wondering frantically how much he had betrayed. Then to his relief he heard Elliott's voice behind him, and made his escape into the kitchen.

Mirry was potentially right in her suspicions, he admitted, squaring his shoulders in mental preparation for the ordeal that lay ahead of him. Something would have to be done. But what?

Grimacing to himself, he acknowledged that when it came to matters of plotting and planning he had no tactical skills whatsoever, which meant that he would have to go back upstairs and tell Mirry that she had been right and that he was wrong.

Rosy stood facing the window, admiring the view it gave over Bea's beautiful gardens. Strange to think that less than three months ago she had had no idea that Elliott and Bea existed . . . that she had any family at all apart from Great-Aunt Maud. And then her aunt had died, and it was only when she was clearing out the huge, old-fashioned desk, which no one had been allowed to touch during her aunt's lifetime, that Rosy had discovered the truth.

Her grandmother, pregnant and disgraced, had been cast off by her family. She had come to the tiny Northumberland village of Hopesly in response to an advertisement for a housekeeper and had got the job. She had apparently kept her condition a secret until the day she had fallen on the stairs and lost the baby. Rosy had wept a little over that pitiful entry in her grandmother's diary, made so many days after those telling empty pages. She had expected to be dismissed from her job, but instead Major Savage had kept her on.

They had married less than a year later. Not a love match, as her grandmother had confided to her diary, but a good marriage for all that, and Rosy's mother had been born two years after that. Reading the diaries, it had come across to Rosy how much her grandmother had missed her family, and especially her brother, but she had never once made any attempt to get in touch with them.

The terrorist bomb in Spain which had killed her grandparents and parents had left Rosy in the sole charge of her great-aunt, and Rosy had had no idea until her death that any other family existed.

At first she hadn't known what she should do; her grandfather had been a wealthy man and Rosy had inherited everything he owned. She had had a university education, but had never worked, because by the time she got her degree her great-aunt's health was failing and she had returned home to repay her for the care which she herself had so unstintingly given to Rosy.

She had reasoned with herself that such a long-ago scandal, so unimportant by modern-day standards, would surely no longer be a barrier separating her from her grandmother's family, and so she had applied to her solicitor for advice, asking him if it were possible to trace her mother's mother's family.

He had confirmed that it was, but it had still been a surprise less than a month later to receive a letter from him, informing her that she had a second cousin, Elliott Chalmers, and then going on to detail the extremely complex family relationship which linked Elliott Chalmers to the Bellaire family of which his wife was a member. Reading the letter, Rosy had had a sudden forlorn sense of being very alone, and very envious of this second cousin of hers, who possessed such a myriad and apparently fascinating set of relatives.

The situation was an odd one. Charles and Cressida Bellaire had divorced when their eldest daughter Bea was very young, he to go to Hollywood and she to remain in England and marry Rosy's uncle, Elliott Chalmers' father. There had been a daughter from that marriage, Lucilla, and then, in the oddest quirk of all, after her uncle's death, Charles and Cressida Bellaire had remarried and then gone on to produce four more children:

male twins, Benedict and Sebastian, a daughter, Miranda, and then another son, William.

Rosy had ached to know more about this charismatic and potently fascinating family, entranced by the sound of them and the details her vivid imagination had filled in between the dry lines of her solicitor's letter, as she had been by books as a child.

Her world had always been a lonely one in terms of human companionship. Savage House was quite remote, her parents and grandparents devoting all their time and energy to keeping the estate going and to maintaining the beautiful gardens for which the house was justly famous.

On their deaths it had had to be sold. Luckily the National Trust had taken it over, not because of the house, but because of its gardens, and Rosy had gone to live with Great-Aunt Maud in the Dower House.

She hadn't missed the big house. She preferred the Dower House and she enjoyed the company of her great-aunt, who had a fund of fascinating stories. And so she had grown up not realising how alienated she was from modern society and her peers until she went to university and discovered the disparity in their thinking and her own. Once she had discovered it, she wisely kept the discovery to herself, and gained the reputation of being withdrawn and aloof.

All that had changed now, though, and here, living at the heart of this very special family, she felt like a plant that had been transplanted from the shade to the rich warmth of the sun. She could practically feel herself blossoming. Elliott's wife, Bea, must be one of the nicest, most generous people in the world. She had made her welcome right from the start.

The very day they had received her initial tentative letter of explanation, Bea had telephoned her, inviting her to come down and stay with them. And she had been here ever since.

Bea, still in the early debilitating weeks of pregnancy, had welcomed her offer of assistance with her two small children and Elliott's charity work, normally something they shared, and Rosy couldn't remember a time when she had felt more content.

Of course, she hadn't met the twins yet...nor Lucilla, who was married to an American, but she had met Mirry and William and she liked them both.

Yes, she liked them, but she was well on the way to loving Bea, who was not related to her by blood at all, but for whom she felt an affinity almost approaching that of a sister.

But Rosy wasn't used to showing her feelings; her aunt had been well-meaning and fond of her in her way, but she was also one of the old school, who did not believe in showing physical affection or encouraging others to do so.

It was her view that teenage girls should be discouraged from emotional displays, rather than the other way round, and Rosy already felt frankly envious of the easy way in which Mirry especially was able to discuss what she thought and felt.

She had agonised so much about whether or not to make herself known to Elliott...about whether or not he would welcome her into his life...that she had been almost overwhelmed by the warmth with which Bea had opened her heart and her home to her.

Already Rosy knew exactly why Elliott loved his wife so much and the bond between the two of them was so very strong.

Their relationship was the first of its kind that Rosy had witnessed at first-hand. Her parents had loved one another, but she had been a child of that relationship and had accepted their love for one another with a child's uncaring acceptance of adult emotions.

Now it was different, and she had to confess to the odd pang of envy when she witnessed the very obvious love between Elliott and Bea, and to remind herself that she couldn't stay with them forever...that she must make a decision about her future. Already Bea was coaxing her to let the Dower House and buy something small locally so that she would be near them. A tempting prospect. She picked up the files she had been sorting out. Normally Elliott had a part-time secretary coming in to help him with his charity work, but she had recently been recuperating from an operation, and Rosy had offered to step into the breach until she returned. The trouble was that she was becoming almost too much at home here with Elliott and Bea; like a little mole, she was inclined to tunnel and dig for herself a cosy little hiding-place where she felt secure. And she did feel secure here.

There might, she acknowledged fair-mindedly, be other single girls of her age, twenty-five, coming up for twenty-six, who might find her life dull, devoid as it was of romance...of men...but during her time at university Rosy had been made forcibly and uncomfortably aware of how far behind her peers she lagged in terms of sexual experience.

It had been too late then to regret the many absorbingly happy hours spent with her parents and grandparents, tending the gardens of Savage House, listening while her grandfather and father discoursed on the progress of their experimental flock of wool-bearing sheep; and it was much, much too late now.

It was all very well for the media to proclaim that a new mood of conscious and careful chastity prevailed, but Rosy was acutely conscious of the fact that any intimate relationship with a man was bound to lead to the kind of explanations she had begun to dread during her university days.

Her virginity was something that surely these days she could lose without comment or notice from a practical point of view, but her almost total lack of experience...a lack which had already once been humiliatingly underlined and mocked...that was something there was just no way she could hide.

Even now, her pale skin flushed betrayingly at the memory of that stocky, vital Welsh undergraduate who had laid siege to her, and then dropped her with embarrassing speed the moment he realised her inexperience, telling her quite bluntly that there was no place in his life for the encumbrance of a girl who didn't know the right moves...the way the game was played.

After that, she had refused all the dates that came her way, petrified of being rejected again, and then, when her great-aunt had become ill and she had been needed at home—well, it had been easy then to forget her humiliation and to concentrate on the hundred and one tasks that occupied her days.

Now, though, it wasn't so easy. She was almost twenty-six, a slender, smallish blonde with serious grey eyes and a smooth pageboy haircut that brushed her shoulders and added to her air of grave calm. She was slim without being thin, her features neat and even, apart from her mouth. That had a sensual, uncharacteristic fullness that made men focus on her speculatively, until she looked coolly at them, dismissing their mental fantasies.

Yes, she was happier now than at any time since losing her parents, and yet . . . and yet there were odd, fleeting instances when by accident she intercepted a look that Bea and Elliott exchanged . . . a look of intimacy and love that totally excluded her and made her sharply aware that the physical body was not designed for complete solitude.

These hormonal and emotional outbreaks of rebellion were speedily dealt with; all it took was five minutes on her own, and total recall of her humiliating dismissal by Gareth Holmes.

She sighed faintly, and realised she was standing daydreaming when she ought to be checking through these files for an all-important name and address.

In addition to his own work, Elliott had taken on the responsibility of treasurer of a locally based charity, involved in raising funds for the establish-

ment of shelters in large cities which provided overnight accommodation for the homeless.

Working with him on it had given her a fascinating insight into Elliott's complex character.
Outwardly tough and, to the uninitiated, cynical,
Elliott had an extremely compassionate and caring
heart...

She had become extremely attached to her second
cousin during the short time she had known him,
and even more attached to his wife, Bea, who right
from the start had treated her as fondly as another
sister, mothering her... spoiling her... loving her,
Rosy acknowledged ruefully.

This evening, though, she had been conscious of
a slight air of constraint in William and Mirry's
manner towards her, and she was beginning to
wonder if she had perhaps outstayed her welcome.
Bea's pregnancy, although progressing well as far
as the twins were concerned, was having a very debilitating effect on her.

'The same thing happened with both my others,'
Bea had assured her, when Rosy had expressed
concern for her pale face and wan appearance. 'By
the time I get to four or five months I'll start to
pick up.'

And since William had arrived for a half-term
visit, followed by Miranda, who was taking a break
from Chichester, where the costume design
company she had started was involved in making
costumes for a couple of major productions, Rosy
had been even more conscious of how much Bea's
family drained her and took her for granted, and
she had been wondering if she herself wasn't guilty

of exactly the same thing...basking in the love that Bea gave so freely, without thought for its giver.

One or two acid little remarks Miranda had made about married couples needing time on their own had found their mark, although Bea had been the first to chide her youngest sister, and point out to her that Rosy was an invaluable help to Elliott.

But only this morning Elliott's secretary had phoned to say she could return to work at the end of the week, and, much as she was loath to do so, Rosy was wondering if she ought not to terminate her visit and return home.

To a house which was far too large for one person, and far too remote to live in alone? She was desperately tempted to either sell it or let it and look for something smaller...here in Gloucester-shire, which she had already come to love...

Because living here meant that she would be close to Bea and Elliott and their family, or for its own sake? Surely she was far too old to need to cling to such a distant family connection?

Was one ever too old? Rosy asked herself wryly. Perhaps the fact that her own family ties had been severed when she was at such a vulnerable age, and so tragically, had something to do with the fact that she still had this inner yearning for roots, for stability, for family.

Well, there was no one else to make the decision for her. The grandfather clock that was Bea's pride and joy chimed the half-hour and she put down the files. She had promised Henrietta that she would help her with dinner. It meant that Bea was free to have a rest, and Elliott, solicitous husband that he was, normally ensured that she did so by making the hour before dinner sacrosanct to them both by sweeping his wife off to her small private sitting-room and very firmly closing the door against anyone else, a practice of which both Henrietta and Rosy fully approved.

Her hands were grubby from the files, and so, instead of going straight to the kitchen, she went upstairs first to the very pretty guest-room which had its own bathroom, which Bea had given her. It was right at the end of the landing, and to reach it she had to walk past the open door to Miranda's room.

The other girl was already inside it. Rosy could hear her speaking to someone, and then she froze as she heard her own name mentioned.

'See, I knew I was right. Rosy is after Elliott,' Mirry announced furiously, pacing up and down her bedroom floor as she listened to William's muttered admission. 'I told you what was going on, but you wouldn't listen to me...' She wheeled round abruptly and faced her brother. 'We've got to do something, William. I suppose you ought to say something to Elliott. You *are* Bea's brother, after all.'

William stuttered a strangled protest, and Miranda frowned, acknowledging that her socially inept brother was hardly one to tackle the urbane and rather formidable Elliott on a subject of such delicacy. She would have done it herself, but she suspected that Elliott would soon run rings round her with some sophisticated argument. And then, of course, there was the matter of the thirty-five thousand pounds he had lent her when she set up in business on her own last year.

'All right then, but you do agree we've got to get rid of Rosy—for Bea's sake. It's obvious she's fallen for Elliott, and . . .'

Outside, Rosy winced, stunned with shock and pain, totally unable to move; and then, recovering, she was tempted to thrust open the door and go in and confront them, until she discovered that she was actually trembling and that silly tears were clouding her eyes. Of course, it was only natural that they should want to defend their sister's marriage, but for them to actually think . . . She had never dreamed how her burgeoning relationship with Elliott was being misconstrued. So Miranda thought she was 'after him'. She trembled with indignation. She had never pursued a man in her life, and never would pursue a married one—Elliott was her cousin, for heaven's sake!

Admittedly Miranda had been a little aloof with her right from the start, but she had foolishly thought it was because Mirry was a little jealous of her relationship with Bea, never guessing that she suspected Rosy was trying to start an affair with Elliott. An affair . . . the very word made her feel ashamed and grubby . . . and hurt. She liked Elliott, yes, but as a cousin . . . and if Mirry had the slightest bit of sense she would realise that nothing could destroy the relationship that Bea and Elliott shared.

She heard William make some inarticulate comment, and something made her hold back, even though she knew she ought to walk in and confront the pair of them.

'Well, you know what you've got to do,' Mirry was saying firmly. 'You must invite Rosy to spend a few days in Oxford with you. After all, you've got masses of spare room in that house you share. Why on earth Elliott actually bought a house in Oxford I'll never know.'

'Good investment,' William told her patiently. 'We all pay him rent, and then if I stay on to get my doctorate...'

'Oh, yes, but let's keep to the point, shall we?' Mirry demanded, growing impatient. 'You've got to persuade Rosy that she ought to spend a few days in Oxford. And then, when you've got her there, all you've got to do is to make sure you introduce her to masses of men...that's bound to take her mind off Elliott. I mean, I'm sure a lot of it must be propinquity,' Mirry said fair-mindedly. 'I don't think she really wants to hurt Bea. She probably just can't help herself, but once she's got someone else to take her mind off Elliott...'

Outside the door, Rosy's eyes widened in indignation and a certain degree of grim amusement. She and Mirry were virtually the same age, but so very different in character. Mirry fell in and out of love like a child falling into puddles, Elliott had once remarked a little unkindly, and, although the other girl wasn't shallow by any means, Rosy realised that emotionally they were almost two different species.

William was talking again, muttering something about not being sure how he was going to persuade her to go to Oxford. Outside, Rosy gave a grim smile. It would be very pleasant to teach them both a lesson by repeating her eavesdropping at the dinner-table tonight, and then she remembered her grandfather once making a sage comment after a dinner party where one of the female guests had been tormented unmercifully by the deliberate flirtation of another woman with her husband.

The man concerned had been oblivious to what was going on and totally devoted to his wife, but, as her grandfather had said at the time, from a tiny insecurity a great tree of doubt and misery could grow. Bea wasn't feeling well, and while Rosy felt quite sure that Bea knew quite well that Elliott was very much in love with her, mightn't she perhaps start wondering if Rosy's obvious affection for Elliott was quite as innocent as Rosy might claim?

She would hate any kind of barrier to grow between Bea and herself. She would hate to be responsible for any kind of unhappiness, however fleeting, for the other woman, and in the circumstances, much as she would have loved to punish the two wrong-headed plotters she could hear but not see, she felt she had little alternative but to let the whole thing go.

Perhaps now would be a good time for her to announce that it was time for her to go home. Once there, she could then decide what she intended to do with the rest of her life. Once she had gone, William and Mirry would stop worrying about their sister's marriage, and, if she did decide to sell the Dower House and return to Gloucestershire, then it would be to a home of her own where she couldn't be accused of trying to steal another woman's husband.

Angry and hurt, she hurried into her own bedroom, washed her hands, and then went back downstairs to the kitchen to help Henrietta.

'Cat got your tongue, then?' Henrietta asked her, after they had worked side by side in silence for almost half an hour. Henrietta had given her grudging approval to Elliott's second cousin, a rare accolade given to few.

'I was just thinking that it's time I went home,' Rosy told her quietly, deliberately not looking at her. Henrietta was extremely shrewd and she knew, because Rosy had told her, just how happy she was here.

She suspected that Henrietta would have questioned her more deeply, but William came into the kitchen, asking hopefully if there was anything to eat. Rosy noticed sadly that he avoided looking directly at her. She liked William, and she had thought he liked her.

CHAPTER TWO

'Go to Oxford with you? But William...what on earth would Rosy do there? She doesn't know anyone and, according to you, you're at lectures all day long...'

Bea stared at her youngest brother in exasperation, totally astounded by his dinner-table suggestion that Rosy might like to go back with him when he returned to Oxford.

'Oh, Bea, of course she must go,' Mirry interrupted eagerly. 'She'll love it. All those men...' She rolled her eyes and glared at Rosy, hiding the glower behind a wide smile.

'Mirry, unlike you, Rosy's every thought is not preoccupied with men,' Bea told her sister with a touch of asperity. Without knowing what had caused it, Bea was acutely aware of Mirry's underlying hostility towards Rosy and she couldn't understand it. Rosy was such a darling, so kind and gentle, so marvellous with the children. So much the sister she had always longed for and never had. Someone with whom she could share her thoughts in a way she never had with anyone else. She would miss her dreadfully if she were to leave.

'Elliott, tell William that this suggestion's ridiculous,' Bea implored, turning to her husband and then adding, flushing a little when he remained silent, 'Heavens, Rosy will begin to think we're trying to get rid of her...'

'I hope not,' Elliott said thoughtfully, surveying the downbent heads of his brother- and sister-in-law. 'But, as it happens, I think William's idea is a good one.'

Both Beatrice and Rosy focused on him. He smiled at his wife first, a loving, reassuring smile that made her mouth tremble a little, and then at Rosy, a gentle, almost paternal smile that made Rosy's heart suddenly lurch on an agonised wave of horror. Surely *Elliott* didn't think that she'd got some kind of idiotic crush on him?

As Elliott continued to look at her, her uncomfortable suspicion became a horrid certainty that lodged round her heart like a lump of ice. Suddenly it was all she could do not to push her plate away and run out of the room. She had never thought of that... She was torn between tears and embarrassment. How stupid of her to assume that Elliott would just *know* that her feelings for him were fraternal. How embarrassing for him this whole situation was if he thought she did have a crush on him...a crush which his very cool look was telling her quite plainly that he did not return.

She went hot and cold all over, and to her shock, instead of announcing firmly and calmly, as she had intended to do, that she was going to go home, she heard herself gabbling a muddled acceptance of William's invitation and then compounding her folly by announcing that Oxford was one of the places she had always wanted to visit and that there was nothing she would like more than to take advantage of William's generous invitation.

It was Bea's doubtful and rather hurt, 'Well, of course, if you're sure . . .' that broke the silence that followed.

Far too triumphantly, or so it seemed to Rosy's sensitive ears, Mirry crowed, 'There you are, Bea. I told you. I bet she's dying to get there and meet tons of new men . . .'

From the other side of the table, Elliott was saying calmly, 'I'm sure you'll enjoy yourself, Rosy. It will do you good to socialise a bit more . . . I'm afraid Bea and I have become extremely insular and very married of late. Very pleasant for a happily married couple, but rather dull for a young woman.'

Rosy opened her mouth to contradict him and then closed it again. Anything she said now could only make the situation worse. While she tried grimly to finish her meal, she was aware of arrangements being made around her, and suddenly realised that it had apparently been decided that, when William returned to Oxford, she would go with him. Since he had no car and she did, it seemed the most sensible solution, saving him a dull train journey.

Bea was still protesting that everything seemed to have been decided very quickly, but no one was listening to her.

Mirry was chattering on about May Balls, announcing that Rosy was bound to need to buy stacks of new clothes, and in all the hubbub Rosy could only hope that her own silence and misery would go unnoticed.

That Elliott should be thinking along similar lines to William and Mirry was just something that had never entered her head. She felt horribly let down by him...hurt, distraught almost that he could think her so self-centred and emotionally immature. Of course she admired and liked him...but only as the cousin she had never known she had.

But she wasn't going to plead for his understanding, like a criminal at the bar, she decided grimly. If he actually thought that she was in danger of developing a crush on him, then going to Oxford was probably one of the best things she could do.

What would be even better, she acknowledged tiredly later, in bed and unable to sleep, would have been if she had sensibly announced her intentions of returning home.

And then an unfamiliar and rather immature voice added, surely rather shockingly, that what would be best of all would be if she found herself a man in Oxford, whom she could flaunt in front of Mirry and William and Elliott as proof that their suspicions were completely unfounded.

Oddly, enough, it was on that thought that she eventually fell asleep.

She wasn't the only member of the household to go to bed with an uneasy conscience.

William, invading his sister's bedroom to find her sitting cross-legged in bed, her face covered in some repulsive sticky goo, her nose stuck in the pages of a book of historical costume, a plate of Henrietta's jam tarts conveniently to hand, eyed the plate thoughtfully and then sat down opposite her, reaching for one and saying firmly, 'I think you were wrong about Elliott. He seemed quite keen for Rosy to come to Oxford.'

In point of fact, William was beginning to feel quite sorry for Rosy. He liked her and had done right from the start, and she had looked quite haunted tonight.

'Mm... That's just a smokescreen,' Mirry said darkly, putting down her book. 'Either that, or he's beginning to realise the danger he's in. I never said that he *didn't* love Bea,' she said virtuously. 'But he *is* a man, and men are always vulnerable where women are concerned.'

William made a derisive snort and said 'Much you know,' which caused Mirry to abandon her lofty pose and hit him on the head with her book.

'Well, I know a lot more about it than you do,' she told him belligerently. 'And it's no good trying to wriggle out of our agreement. I'd have invited her back to Chichester with me, but there just isn't room.'

William knew this was true. Rooms in Chichester were at a premium during the festival, and Mirry shared a tiny cottage in a village several miles away with her partner and the three girls who worked for them, plus three extremely old-fashioned and large industrial sewing-machines, a dog and two cats... No, there was no room for Rosy there.

'You've got to introduce her to as many men as you can. Take her to one of those lunch thing-ummies your tutors give...'

William pulled a face, and grimaced as Mirry flipped her book at the hand he had stretched out for the last jam tart.

'That's mine,' she told him firmly.

'Greedy pig. It's a wonder you aren't hugely fat.'

'Look who's talking...'

They bickered amicably for another half-hour or so until Mirry started to yawn and told her brother that she wanted to go to sleep.

In their own room at the opposite end of the house, having checked that both their son and daughter were safely asleep, Bea slid into bed beside her husband.

'Elliott, why do you want Rosy to go?' she asked him quietly. 'She looked so... so hurt and lost, I could have cried for her.'

'I know. But she needs something we can't give her, Bea. She needs to go out and meet people. I've been making a few discreet enquiries. She's led one hell of an isolated existence. First with her parents and grandparents, and then later, after university, with her great-aunt.

'She's a very attractive and intelligent young woman of twenty-five who, if she isn't pushed a little, will end up a very lonely human being. Now, I know people for whom that would be no burden at all, but not Rosy. She needs people... she needs to love and be loved, even if she herself doesn't realise it yet. I've been wondering for the last few days how on earth we could get her involved with other people. These two...' he patted his wife's stomach fondly, 'mean that any activities in that direction on our part have to be curtailed at the moment. I must admit I'd never thought of sending her off to Oxford with William, but it's almost the ideal solution.'

'You expect *William* to introduce her to people?' Bea asked him, astounded.

'You're doing your brother an injustice. William may not be the most articulate creature in the world, but he's no idiot. Four of them share that house, don't they? William has far too highly a developed sense of responsibility—something you've taught him—to forget that Rosy is there at his invitation. He might hate doing it, but he'll shepherd her round like the good sheepdog he is, and Rosy, bless her heart, is far too kind-hearted to tell him that socialising is the very last thing she wants to do.'

'Yes. Did you notice the way she shuddered when Mirry kept going on about her meeting loads of men?'

'Mm.'

Ignoring the tone of voice that indicated that it was not a subject he wished to pursue, Bea continued thoughtfully, 'I wonder why. She's so very lovely...'

'Very lovely,' her husband agreed blandly, making her frown at him, until he added wryly, 'Rather withdrawn and, unless I'm very much mistaken, extremely unawakened. When that dawns on our William, as I fear it must, I suspect that any would-be seducer is going to find himself with the devil of a job on his hands. As I just said, William can be extremely sheepdoggish, and, just in case that maternal heart of yours is already pitter-pattering with anxiety on Rosy's behalf, I think you can rest assured that William will prove more than adept at guarding your little lamb from the wolves.'

'Know it all, don't you?' Bea demanded with more than a touch of asperity.

'If not all, then a good ninety-nine per cent,' Elliott told her smugly, grinning at her. 'One thing does puzzle me a little, though. I hadn't expected Rosy to give in so easily.'

'Perhaps she *wants* to go to Oxford,' Bea suggested.

'Mm . . . the same way a nervous swimmer wants to swim the Channel,' Elliott agreed drily, reaching out to switch off the lamp as Bea snuggled down beside him.

Accommodatingly he made room for her and the slight bump which was to be the newest addition to their family.

'What's it going to be this time?' he asked her softly, as he kissed her.

'Boys, I think,' Bea whispered back. 'Then next time we could try for two girls . . .'

'What?'

'You said you wanted a large family,' Bea reminded him, hiding her smile.

'Four *is* a large family, especially when one-half of it is represented by twins,' Elliott told her firmly.

Beatrice said nothing. Twin boys and then twin girls . . . Six was such a nice, even number.

'Are you sure you've got everything? And, Rosy, if you don't like Oxford . . .'

Elliott put a hand on Bea's arm and drew her back from the open window of the car. 'She will like it,' he told her calmly, adding, 'Drive carefully, Rosy. Don't let William bully you into speeding... Nor into letting him drive.'

William grimaced and flushed a little. Elliott had taught him to drive, and on their first time out he had almost dented Elliott's new car, something he suspected he was never going to be allowed to forget.

Mirry had already gone, rushing back to Chichester in a whirlwind of kisses and hugs, demanding promises from them all that they would come to see 'her' productions.

Rosy deliberately turned away as Elliott bent to kiss her, so that the brief caress went wide of her cheek. She saw the enigmatic look he gave and returned it with a proudly disdainful stare.

Only with Bea could she be anything approaching natural, and tears stung her eyes as Bea kissed her fondly and impressed upon her that she would miss her dreadfully.

'I know it's only for a week, but already I'm longing for it to be over.'

Only a week... Rosy wasn't so sure. She had already made up her mind that as soon as she decently could she would make her excuses to William and go home.

It didn't take them long to reach Oxford. William proved to be an excellent navigator, and never once made any male judgements about her driving.

The house he lived in was just outside the city, a stately terrace with six bedrooms on the two upper storeys, and a good-sized sitting-room, dining-room and communal kitchen on the ground floor.

She was introduced to the rest of the quartet who shared the house with him: two other young men, Tom and Alan, and a girl, Chrissie, who surveyed her blonde elegance with openly envious eyes and announced that she was the token woman in an otherwise male household.

None of them seemed to find anything odd in the fact that William had brought her back with him, but as Rosy quickly discovered, as she listened to their light-hearted bantering and made mental plans to quickly make her excuses to return home, it wasn't going to be that easy.

'Lucky you, having a car,' Chrissie commented enviously. 'We're a bit stuck here without one. We have to make do with our bikes...' She pulled a face, and then said to William, 'I hope you're going to Richard's lunch tomorrow. You've missed out on the last four, and he made a sarky comment about it the last time.'

Rosy quickly learned that Richard Donovan was one of William's tutors, and that the lunch Chrissie was referring to was a monthly event at which his students were supposed to put in an appearance, and somehow or other, without really knowing how it had happened, she discovered that she had agreed not only to drive Chrissie and William to the lunch party but also to attend it with them.

'You'll cause quite a stir,' Chrissie warned her. 'Richard is rather a sucker for blondes. He'll make a beeline for you, and then Mrs D will drag him off. She always does.' She gave a mock shudder.

'Goodness, imagine what a marriage like that must be like. Awful. Pity Gorgeous George is away at the moment...' She rolled her eyes theatrically. 'Now there's a man who thinks he's God's gift.'

'Cat,' William tugged her hair and teased. 'Just because he doesn't fancy you...'

'Oh, yeah. That's all you know. Last year——'

'Break it up, you two,' Alan interrupted. 'I'm hungry. Whose turn is it for kitchen duties?'

'Not mine,' Tom assured them, adding, 'and besides, I've got a date.'

'I suppose that means you've already cleared out the fridge and it's empty,' Chrissie complained.

'Look—er—why don't I take you all out for dinner?' Rosy suggested, surprising herself a little. She had had no intention of prolonging the farce of staying with William, and yet, now that she was here, for some reason she was allowing herself to be carried along on the flow of their lives, and enjoying it!

'Great idea,' Chrissie said enthusiastically. 'I suppose it's too much to hope that you like Italian.'

Assuring her gravely that it wasn't, Rosy waited patiently while they all piled into her car.

The evening was so much of a success that she was sorry when it came to an end. Her anger against William had faded completely, and instead of driving home in the morning, as she had planned, it seemed that she would be going with Chrissie and William to attend their lunch party.

It wouldn't be a dressy affair, Chrissie assured her. With so many student guests, all of them on grants, it was hardly likely to be, and so Rosy dressed in a plain linen dress she had had for years but which she felt comfortable in, and with it she wore a soft short-sleeved cotton knitted sweater. It was a warm day and the outfit was stylishly cool, setting her apart from the student body in their imaginative assortment of what looked at first glance like a collection of black dusters.

The Donovans' house was on the opposite side of Oxford, a four-square Victorian mansion, of what Rosy privately considered a rather pretentious stylishness, a view which was reinforced by Helen Donovan, a tall, rather overpowering woman who looked rather sharply at her when William introduced her, and gave her a tight, cold smile.

There was a buffet lunch out in the dining-room, and despite the fact that french windows stood open to the garden no one seemed to be taking advantage of its cool greenness. It wasn't a hot day, but nevertheless it was warm enough to tempt Rosy outside, when she realised that William was deeply involved in a discussion that was way over her head. Excusing herself with a smile, she sauntered towards the door.

Groups of animated students argued volubly all around her; their involvement and earnestness amused her a little. Had she herself ever been that young? She supposed she must have been... once.

The garden was too well-manicured for her taste, but beyond the formality of the clipped lawn and immaculate flowerbeds she could see a small orchard. She walked towards it. The long double perennial border at home would just be coming up to its best. It had been planted by her great-great-grandmother and was reputed to be one of the best of its kind... She missed the garden, where she didn't miss the house. A hedge separated this garden from the orchard. There was a gate in it, and she opened it, and breathed deeply as she walked through. This was better. Grass... stunted apple trees... tranquillity. It felt wonderful to be alone. Only she wasn't alone...

There was a man sitting under one of the trees. No, not sitting, exactly: he was in a wheelchair. Impossible from this distance to say how old he was. His skin was bleached of all colour, his body thin. He looked as though he was tall. He had a short and totally unflattering haircut. His dark hair seemed to stick up in untidy tufts. He was wearing glasses, and as she watched he turned his head and saw her.

Guiltily aware that she had invaded his privacy, Rosy stammered an excuse for disturbing him and tried to back out of the small glade.

'It's all right. I'd just reached the stage where I was beginning to get bored with my own company. Please don't go. Come and tell me what you're doing here instead. You're not one of Richard's students, are you?'

'No,' Rosy agreed. 'I'm here with a... relative.'

He was younger than she had first imagined, somewhere in his mid-thirties, and pitifully thin, she realised on a wave of compassion. He either was or had been very ill, she acknowledged, recognising the symptoms of wasting that had attacked his frame.

'I see. And this relative *is*, I take it, one of Richard's students.'

'Yes,' she acknowledged. There was nowhere for her to sit other than at his feet and, because it seemed kinder than standing over him looking down at him, she did so, not noticing the look he gave her.

'And he's brought you here as some form of penance, has he?'

'Not exactly.' Suddenly all her anger came back, and she said with more frankness than was normal for her, 'He's brought me here to try and find me a man.' There was a moment's pause while he studied her set shoulders and proudly held head thoughtfully, without her being aware of the scrutiny.

'Has he, indeed?' he murmured at last. She turned round and looked at him. He looked very worn down, and she wondered guiltily if she was tiring him, if he had come here, as she had, to escape from the rest of the human race.

She made to get up but he stopped her, touching her lightly on her shoulder.

'You can't go now, not after that extremely intriguing statement. Sit down and tell me all about it.'

And for some reason Rosy discovered that that was exactly what she wanted to do. Perhaps it was the calming, soothing effect of his voice...perhaps it was the garden, reminding her of her home and her family; or perhaps it was just the man himself, and his aura of kindness...the awareness she had of his suffering and his concern for humanity... things she could not have put into words... mere sensations, feelings.

She told him as briefly as she could, unaware of the anger and pain shadowing her voice.

'Pathetic, isn't it?' she said when she finished, turning round to look at him.

His face was in the shadows, his eyes impossible to read. 'Not pathetic... a little sad. It's always sad when the purest human motives are misunderstood. It also posed one or two interesting anomalies. And now you've told me so much about yourself, I think you and I should introduce ourselves. I'm Callum Blake.'

'Rosy Seton.'

'So, Rosy Seton, and what do you do when you're not accompanying your relatives to dull academic lunches?' She frowned for a moment, and he explained, 'How do you earn your living?'

'I don't. I took my degree several years ago, and got some additional secretarial qualifications, but my aunt became ill... I went home to take care of her, and now... Well, now I suppose I ought to look for a job, although they aren't easy to come by in the north. I had thought of letting the house, and moving down here, although quite who is going to employ me, and as what, I really have no idea.'

'I have,' Callum told her quietly, watching her steadily and again she stared at him. For such a very frail man, he had a surprisingly commanding voice. 'You, Rosy Seton, are, I suspect, the answer to all my prayers.'

'What?' She frowned, wondering what he meant.

'Now it's my turn for explanations.' He moved uncomfortably in his wheelchair, and Rosy, realising that the sun was shining directly into his eyes, got up and moved the chair as she had often had to do for her great-aunt.

'Thanks.' He gave her a smile that heart-breakingly illuminated the thinness of his face. 'This wheelchair isn't a permanency, thank goodness. More of a convenience. It's surprising the effect it tends to have on people. Surprising, and often a little depressing.

'Since I've been in it, I've come to realise that there's far more than one kind of discrimination, and I must say I shan't be sorry when the time comes for me to part company with it.'

'What happened?' Rosy asked him softly, sensing that he wouldn't mind her asking.

'I was out in Ethiopia studying the effects of the famine. That's my subject—world economics. I was shot by a band attacking one of the food trains, and then, when I was travelling through Nigeria, I picked up a fever... There isn't enough medication out there for those who need it, never mind those who don't, but there was a hiccup in communications and it was some time before they could ship me back home. By then the bug had taken hold of me in a big way.'

He got out of the chair and limped over to her in an ungainly, uncoordinated fashion.

'As you can see, I'm virtually back on my feet...virtually, but not quite.' He grimaced a little, and she suspected that the movement had caused him pain.

'Like Richard Donovan, I'm a lecturer...in economics. Twelve months ago, I'd decided to take a sabbatical. Go out to Ethiopia and see how economics actually work. Now I'm writing a series of articles about what I learned. I need someone to help me work on them and to help me with the preparation of a series of lectures I intend to give. I think you could be that someone. Would the job appeal?'

Rosy knew that it would. She liked this man, felt drawn to him, found him completely unintimidating and easy to be with.

'Very much,' she told him honestly, with a smile. 'Although I suspect this is a rather unorthodox way to recruit an employee!'

'That depends on the employee and the employer. From what I've learned about you so far, I should say that we'd work exceptionally well together.'

Rosy liked the way he described her work for him as a partnership, and her heart lifted a little, warmed for the first time since that horrible moment when she had looked at Elliott and realised that he wanted her to leave. Even so, she felt bound to protest a little self-consciously, 'You're offering me a job and you hardly know a thing about me...'

'I know that you appear to be an eminently sensible young woman. You must be if you prefer the tranquillity of the garden to the inside of the house. I'm afraid Helen's taste is rather heavily influenced by the prevailing fashion. I also know that you don't seem to find the sight of this rather unappealing flesh of mine too repulsive. Or at least, if you do, you manage to hide it very well.'

He looked steadily at her, and Rosy returned his look with grave concentration and then said quietly, 'When my great-aunt first became ill, I found it very hard to come to terms with what was happening to her, but she remained so very much herself in spirit that, by sheer effort of will, she made people forget the destruction of her body.'

'A rare gift.' He went back to his chair and sat down in it, and then said bluntly, 'Just in case you're wondering, you won't be required to undertake any nursing duties where I'm concerned. My doctors assure me that by the end of the summer I should be back on my feet permanently, and, quite honestly, the last thing I want at the moment is someone fussing over me in an excess of maternal zeal. Another reason I think you and I will work well together. You don't strike me as the type of person who fusses. Here's my address,' he told her, handing her a small printed card. 'If you could come round tomorrow morning, we can discuss the whole thing further. That will give you a night to sleep on it.'

'And you,' Rosy told him, but to her surprise he shook his head and said firmly,

'I don't need to sleep on it. You're exactly what I want. Ah, I think our idyll is about to be interrupted,' he remarked in an oddly dry voice, and as she turned her head Rosy saw her hostess hurrying towards them.

Her face looked uncomfortably flushed, and from the look she gave her Rosy could see that

Helen Donovan was none too pleased to find her with Callum.

Ignoring Rosy, she hurried to Callum's side, effectively standing between them.

'Callum, my dear, I'm so sorry you've been neglected like this. Why don't you let me wheel you back to the house? You must be bored out of your mind out here.'

'Helen, if you don't mind, I think perhaps I'll go home.' And then, as the older woman made to go to his wheelchair, he added firmly, 'No, that's all right. I mustn't take up any more of your time. Rosy will escort me to my car, won't you, Rosy?'

'Yes, of course.'

Ignoring the angry glare she was being given, Rosy went to stand behind him.

'There's a gate in the hedge just over there. We can get out that way...'

Rosy found it quite easily, but to her surprise, when they reached it, Callum stopped her and got out of the wheelchair, telling her wryly, 'We all have our pride. I think I can make it from here to the car.'

'Which one is it?' Rosy asked him, inspecting the long line of cars parked alongside the road.

'This one.' He indicated a large, comfortable-looking Mercedes, and then delved in his pocket to produce the keys.

Rosy watched as he unlocked the boot doors, helping him to fold the chair and stow it inside.

'Don't forget... Tomorrow morning, say ten-thirty,' he reminded her as he drove away.

It took Rosy several minutes to find William in the crush of students milling through the house.

'Oh, there you are,' he greeted her, frowning slightly at her. 'What happened? I've been looking everywhere for you.'

In case she'd escaped and gone back to Elliott? Rosy wondered grimly.

'I know where she was,' Chrissie announced gleefully, materialising at their sides. 'She was in the garden, talking to Callum. I know because I heard Mrs D complaining like mad to Ricky about it. Snaffling her prize exhibit and then keeping him all to herself. Naughty Rosy...'

'Callum was here—and I missed him?' William looked exceedingly aggrieved. 'I've managed to get on one of his courses next term if he's well enough to come back. What did he say to you, Rosy?' he asked her. 'Did he talk to you about Ethiopia?'

'Only briefly.'

'There was a terrific fuss when he announced that he was taking a sabbatical and going out there. You'd have thought the world had come to an end.'

'So it did, practically... as far as economics lectures were concerned,' William said gloomily. 'Callum is a brilliant lecturer.'

Chrissie pulled a face and, while the two of them were arguing, Rosy mused on the strange interlude in the garden, wondering if she had been completely mad to accept Callum's offer of a job so impulsively. What had happened to her intention of returning home? Returning home to what, though? The same loneliness she had only just escaped from? There was no way she would ever be able to get a job close enough to be able to live in the Dower House, which meant that she might as well stay here.

She liked Callum. There was something so completely non-sexual and non-threatening about him that she had felt relaxed with him right from the start.

She was not a vain woman, but men normally gave her rather more sexual attention than the one uninterested glance she had received from Callum. She wondered idly if he was homosexual, and then dismissed his private life as none of her concern.

She didn't tell William that Callum had offered her a job until they were on their own later in the evening.

His jaw sagged a little and he stared at her. '*Callum* has asked you to work for him?' he asked her in tones of awe.

Rosy nodded. 'Just as a temporary measure. He needs someone to help him with a series of articles he intends to write about Ethiopia, and the preparatory work for some lectures.'

William gave a soundless whistle and looked at her again. 'Callum Blake is just about *the* best economics lecturer there is,' he told her severely. 'He *never* employs an assistant. He hates having his privacy invaded. He has rooms in college that he uses for his tutorials, but he never allows even his best students inside his home.'

'Perhaps he fancies her,' Tom suggested, coming into the sitting-room munching an apple just as William was in mid-flow.

William broke off to scowl darkly at him, while Chrissie, who was at his heels, said blithely, 'Such heresy! The only thing Callum fancies are long rows of figures, and I don't mean the thirty-four, twenty-two, thirty-six variety, either...'

So he wasn't homosexual then, Rosy reflected, leaving them to their bickering while William gave a spirited defence of his hero, claiming that there was nothing wrong with a man just because he didn't flirt with half the female student body.

As she prepared for bed, she reflected that although she was only a very few years older than William and his peers she felt light-years away from them in outlook and opinion. The years of nursing her great-aunt had matured her, and it now seemed odd to her that she herself had ever been a student, awed by young men such as William and his peers, who now seemed to be little more than endearing, overgrown children. That Welshman who had caused her such pain and humiliation had been about William's age. She fell asleep, trying to imagine what her life would have been like if that incident had never happened; if she had simply matured like her peers, going into adulthood with all the necessary sexual experience and expertise.

CHAPTER THREE

IT APPEARED that William had been quite right when he said that Callum liked his privacy, Rosy reflected, as she followed the directions Callum had given her and discovered that he lived in a remote building which looked as though it had once been a row of two or three separate cottages.

Set against a backdrop of undulating hills, its long, low outline was surprisingly in keeping with its surroundings. The exterior walls were whitewashed, the windows small and dark.

The front of the house was set back from the lane at an angle that prevented Rosy from seeing what lay to the rear. A wooden gate guarded the drive, and she had to get out of the car to open it.

It was a pleasantly mild April day, the sky full of billowing clouds, teased by a wind that didn't seem able to make up its mind which way to blow. As she closed the gate behind her, she stood for a moment watching the cloud shadows darken the surface of a nearby pond. A mother moorhen swam out from the reeds, accompanied by her chicks, all paddling furiously as they battled to keep pace with her.

The air felt cool and clean, the spire of a distant church the only sign of human habitation in sight.

The front door opened as she parked her car. Callum was tall—just as she had thought. He was wearing a shirt that looked several sizes too large for him, and a faded pair of jeans that were also too big.

She frowned as she wondered if they had ever fitted him. If so, he must have been an extremely powerfully built man. She didn't know very many academics, but those she did did not possess the kind of physique that would have filled the shirt Callum had on. Perhaps he liked his clothes too big, she reflected uncertainly as he greeted her, and she smiled back at him.

'It's a lovely spot,' she told him as he ducked his head beneath the lintel to the front door, and she followed him into a surprisingly comfortable sitting-room, where a log fire burned in an old-fashioned inglenook fireplace and a rather battered and ancient marmalade cat lay snoozing on a chair.

'I like it. Would you like a cup of coffee? I was just about to make one.'

'Please.'

Rosy examined her surroundings while he was gone. The sitting-room was furnished with a rather battered and very eclectic collection of furniture, which somehow managed to meld together to give a very comfortable and warm homeliness.

An ancient settee with a softly faded loose cover was stacked with books that made it sag in the middle, and the very pretty sofa-table behind it could scarcely be seen beneath a welter of note-books, pens, pencils and dictaphone equipment.

'I keep promising myself I'll move all this stuff into the study,' Callum told her, walking in carrying a mug of coffee which he handed to her before disappearing back into the kitchen to collect his own. As he rejoined her, he told her, 'The study faces north, though, and at the moment isn't very appealing.'

To Rosy the sitting-room felt very warm, but she noticed how Callum seemed to shiver a little, and tactfully moved closer to the fire so that he could follow her. She didn't notice the look he gave her as she paused to study the cat, who looked back at her with remote yellow eyes.

'Harold came with the house,' he informed her. 'I was forced into keeping him on the strength of his abilities as a mouser.'

'And is he good?' Rosy asked him.

'Unfortunately, yes. Even more unfortunate is his proclivity for producing their corpses at the wrong moment. He dropped one at Helen's feet when she came here on a mercy mission, after which she flatly refused to set foot in the house again.'

Something in his voice made Rosy take a chance and say thoughtfully as she looked up at him, 'It must have taken quite a long time to train him to do that...'

She was rewarded with a slight smile. 'An expenditure of effort that was more than worth while,' he told her.

Over their coffee he chatted to her as he had done the previous afternoon, drawing her out into telling him far more about herself than he was telling her about himself, she realised abruptly, half-way through explaining how lonely her childhood had been; she suddenly became silent.

'I suffered a similar problem,' he told her easily, filling the gap she had left. 'My father was in the army. I was the only child. I grew up in an assortment of different countries that left me with an acute longing for somewhere permanent where I could put down roots. The institutionalised way of life probably also explains my present love of solitude.'

When they had finished their coffee he took her into his study, which was, as he had said, several degrees colder than the sitting-room, although there was a fire burning in the grate. She found it acceptably warm, but she could see Callum shivering, even though he made an effort to hide it from her.

William had told her that, although the university faculty had made strenuous efforts to play down Callum's illness, it had got out, as these things always did; that he had been very close to death, and that it would be many months before he was fully fit.

Today he wasn't using the wheelchair, but Rosy noticed that he paused several times to massage the outside of his right thigh, and she guessed that must have been where the bullet had hit him.

'I'll show you round the house and the garden while you're here,' he offered. 'You might as well make yourself familiar with its layout.'

As she had guessed, the house had originally been three small farmworkers' cottages. Left derelict for many years, they had been converted by the previous owner into the present comfortably spacious home.

Downstairs there was a large kitchen, a good-sized dining-room, which looked as though it was never used, Callum's study, the sitting-room and then a large drawing-room, which again looked as though it was never used.

Here, as in the dining-room, the furnishings were far more formal than in the other rooms, and Callum explained to her that he had bought them from the previous owners. That probably explained why the rooms lacked the homely appeal of the sitting-room and kitchen, in which she had instantly felt relaxed.

Upstairs there were five bedrooms and two bathrooms. Callum indicated the door to his bedroom without opening it. All the other bedrooms were very obviously uninhabited, although furnished. Rosy wondered if anyone had ever shared the house with him. William had exhibited shock and disdain at the mere thought of his ever having had a lover, which corresponded to her own opinion that Callum was one of that rare breed of men, aesthetics to their very soul, who were so totally involved and dedicated to the prime interest in their lives that they simply had no room nor any need for more earthy desires.

Physically Callum certainly bore out the popular image of such a man, with his tall, too-thin frame, and slightly stooped stance.

His face had the hollow, carved-out sharpness of the zealot, and when he talked about his work the eyes behind the shield of his glasses glowed and burned.

She still wasn't quite sure what colour his eyes were, and she frowned a little, curious that she should be interested.

He was saying something about the hours he would require her to work and she tried to concentrate, gasping a little when he mentioned the salary he was prepared to pay her.

'That's far too much,' she protested, and when he stopped and looked at her, one eyebrow slightly raised, his mouth suddenly uncompromisingly grim, she was confused both by the sudden and totally unexpected sensation of having walked into something hard and unyielding where she had expected only marshmallow, and by her own reaction to the conflicting signals she was receiving.

'On the contrary, it's merely a fair wage,' he told her calmly. 'I don't think you can have been listening to me properly, Rosy. There will be days when I shall expect you to work far more than the normal six or seven hours. From what you've told me about yourself I'm assuming that there is no one in your life who might object to that.'

It took her several seconds to catch on, and when she did, aggravatingly, she flushed a little.

'No—no, of course not,' she told him, and was confused when he grimaced and said, surprisingly firmly,

'Rosy, there's no of course about it. You're a very attractive young woman . . .'

'Outwardly, perhaps,' she muttered, unaware that he had heard her until he said calmly,

'And, far more important, inwardly too. If the situation should change, I—er—hope you will let me know. I have no wish to have an aggressive and excitable male pounding on my door demanding to know why I'm keeping you working late into the evening.'

'It won't change,' Rosy told him.

'That sounds an uncompromisingly definite statement.'

'It is,' she told him flatly, scowling a little, but not vouchsafing any further explanations.

'Come and see the garden,' he told her. 'It's one of the reasons I bought the house.'

They spent over an hour wandering round it, and, watching him shiver in the April breeze, Rosy was glad that she had suggested they both wear their jackets. She was almost too warm in hers, but she noticed how Callum always contrived to stand in the warmth of the sun.

The garden was spectacular, breathtakingly so, with its maze of walks and small secret gardens hidden by tall yew hedges, and separated from one another by arbours and trellises of old-fashioned roses.

'I don't look after it myself, unfortunately. I don't have time. A firm of gardeners comes in once a month to keep it in order.'

His face looked pinched and cold, and despite the fact that she was enjoying the fresh air Rosy suggested they went back to the house. She noticed that he was walking far more slowly on the way back then he had when they'd left the house, and she carefully matched her pace to his.

They were almost back when he stumbled slightly, and without thinking about it she reached out to support him, grasping his elbow so that he could lean against her. It shocked her to discover how clear the bone was, barely covered in any flesh at all, surely. He was breathing hard, a hectic flush of fever burning his skin.

'You mustn't try to do too much,' Rosy scolded him gently, and then bit her lip, wondering if she had said the wrong thing, but he merely gave a small ghost of a laugh and shook his head, saying, wryly,

'Yes, Grandmama.' But he didn't move away from her, and under the fingers she had gripped round his wrist to give him further support Rosy could feel the frighteningly fast race of his pulse.

Instinct and experience made Rosy stand still and silent as she waited for him to recover, neither drawing away from him nor fussing over him.

She was standing so close to him that she could feel the tremors as though they were her own, and she had to grit her teeth to stop herself from re-acting to them.

It seemed a long time before he said shakily, 'Thanks . . . I'm OK now.'

Rosy didn't let go of him, though, carefully matching her pace to his as they walked slowly inside.

Once they were in, he moved away from her and Rosy let him go, watching in silence as he limped over to the settee and leaned against it. Despite his outward calmness, she had the feeling she wasn't entirely surprised when he balled his hand into a fist and thumped the unprotesting piece of furniture, swearing savagely.

He had his back to her, but the shortness of his hair revealed the back of his neck and the dark surge of colour building there.

He turned round unexpectedly and caught her looking at him. He ran one hand over his head and grimaced slightly. 'The makeshift hospital they put me in was infested with lice. They shaved the patients' heads every week to keep them at bay.'

Rosy couldn't quite control her shudder.

'Oh, you're perfectly safe,' he told her sharply. 'I'm completely de-infested now. Do you still want the job?' he asked her, his voice suddenly drained. He wasn't looking at her, and Rosy was free to let the compassion she was feeling spill freely through her.

'On one condition,' she told him gravely, wishing for some odd reason he would take his glasses off so that she could see his eyes properly.

'And that is?' He still had his back to her, his voice slightly muffled; where his hands rested on the back of the settee she could see the knuckles pushing whitely through the thin skin.

'That you don't teach Harold to drop mice at my feet,' she told him gravely, and then, while he was still smiling at her, added quietly, 'Would it have a deeply prejudicial effect on our working relationship if I suggested that you ought to spend the rest of the day in bed?'

She smiled whimsically, mentally crossing her fingers. She wanted this job, and he had already told her how much he hated being fussed over, but that attack he had suffered outside had been no mere momentary weakness, no matter how much he might try to pretend it had.

He looked at her for a long time and then said with a wry smile, 'Not on this occasion. My doctor keeps warning me that I want to run before I can walk. According to him, I'm lucky to be alive at all. Lassa fever isn't something...'

'Lassa fever...' Rosy stared at him, going white.

'Oh, it's all right, I'm not contagious.'

'No,' she agreed, a new understanding in her eyes as she looked at his wasted frame, trying to imagine the reserves of mental and physical strength he must have had to combat such a deadly disease.

It was late afternoon when she eventually got back to Oxford, having stayed long enough to assure herself that Callum was well enough to be left on his own. She had not offered to make him a meal, nor insisted on waiting until he was safely in bed, knowing that such feminine fussing would only irritate him.

The house was empty, apart from William, who demanded to know if she had taken the job.

When she told him she had, he said tentatively that if she liked she could continue to live in the house. The problem of finding accommodation wasn't one to which she had given much thought. The job with Callum was only temporary, and if William had no objection to her keeping her room then she was only too delighted to do so.

She told him as much, and was rewarded with one of his rare broad grins.

'Chrissie would kill me if I did anything else,' he told her. 'She says it's going to be heaven having another woman here.'

There was still one more hurdle to be overcome, though, and taking a chance that Bea would answer the phone, Rosy picked up the receiver and dialled their number.

She was in luck. Quickly she explained to Bea what had happened; Bea was both surprised and a little disappointed at her news.

'So you won't be coming back here, then. Oh, dear... I shall miss you.'

Rosy told her that she was intending to keep her room at William's, and asked Bea if she thought Elliott would have any objections. She had already agreed with William that she would pay the same rent as the rest of them, and Bea seemed to find it hard to understand what on earth Elliott was likely to object to.

Rosy didn't enlighten her. Even now she was finding it hard to believe that Elliott had so totally misunderstood her feelings.

She was till hurt by his judgement of her, and when Bea suggested that she ring back later when she could speak to Elliott himself she prevaricated, saying that she was going out.

A couple of hours later, lying on the sofa in her sitting-room with her feet up, ruefully complaining that she was not an invalid, Bea passed on Rosy's message to Elliott, watching him frown a little as he drank his tea.

'Now what's wrong...? You pack the poor girl
off to Oxford with William with totally unseemly
haste, and now, when you hear she's staying there,
you start frowning.'

'How much do you know about this man she's
working for?'

'Nothing, really,' Bea admitted, giving him a
thoughtful look. 'He's an economist. He's recovering from an illness contracted in Africa and
he's offered Rosy a job. She did mention that
William knows him and seems rather in awe of
him...from the way she talked about him, she obviously feels totally confident about working for
him.'

'Mm... It isn't so much Rosy's motives that
concern me—I can understand those easily
enough—but his. What do you think would mo-
tivate a man to ask a woman he's never met before,
and knows virtually nothing about, to come and
work for him?'

Bea's eyes rounded a little. 'Oh...' she said a
little uncertainly.

'Oh, indeed,' Elliott agreed drily. 'You know, my
dear, I really think you could do with a shopping
trip.'

'To Oxford?' Bea asked him, her mouth quivering a little.

'To Oxford,' he agreed wryly, smiling back at
her. 'In fact, I think we'll make a short stay of it.'

'I'll phone William. We can stay with them.'

Elliott gave her a wry look. 'I think not. I'm
getting too old to give up my creature comforts.

The last time we stayed there, as I remember, it was William's turn to cook... I'll book into a hotel. We'll leave it a week or so, though, and see how things go.'

CHAPTER FOUR

DURING the first week she worked for Callum, Rosy's new life began to form an uncertain pattern. On those days when Callum was well enough to work, he dictated to her in the sitting-room, where he could keep warm, and then, at those times when his body reminded him of its weakness and he was forced to rest, Rosy worked in the study, transcribing the notes she had taken, sorting out his files and generally restoring order to her cluttered surroundings.

Quietly and without fuss, and without either of them saying a word about it, she also cosseted Callum, never obviously or in a pushy way, but her compassionate eye noticed all the small things that could be done to make his recuperation easier, and her capable hands did them.

By the end of the week she had fallen into the habit of making an evening meal and staying to eat it with him. Afterwards, relaxed and warmed by the food and the fire, they would talk, and she discovered that Callum had a dry, biting wit that made her laugh. He was obviously a very intelligent man, but he was a very human one as well.

Their arrangement was that, unless he had some urgent work on hand, she would have her weekends free, and yet now that it was Friday evening she was discovering that she was reluctant to leave the cottage and go back to Oxford. She felt safe when she was with Callum . . . unthreatened . . . relaxed . . . protected. Her mouth turned down a little—protected from what?

'What's wrong?' he asked her quietly.

He was remarkably astute, she recognised, smiling at him. Her mouth turned down again as she shrugged.

'Nothing, really. I was just wishing it wasn't the weekend. Mirry rang last night and spoke to William. I think she must have been chivvying him about me, because he announced afterwards that he's arranged to take me to a musical recital tomorrow evening. It's Haydn.'

'And you don't like Haydn?' Callum asked her drily.

She shook her head. 'As a matter of fact, I do, but I don't like being the object of someone else's matchmaking activities. If I wanted a man——' she began indignantly, and then broke off.

'*If* you wanted a man . . . but you don't, do you?' he said succinctly.

'No,' she admitted shortly, turning her head away in an instinctively protective gesture, ducking her chin so that he couldn't see her eyes.

'Want to talk about it?'

There was no pressure in the question . . . no spurious sexual curiosity, no gloating male superiority . . . and then she remembered that he must be used to dealing with the emotional problems of vulnerable undergraduates. More to herself than to him, she murmured, 'Can I?' but he heard her and said quietly,

'Only you know the answer to that one, but, if you want to give it a try, I'm willing to listen.'

He got up from his chair, less clumsily than usual, Rosy thought, absently watching him, measuring the co-ordination of his muscles and the degree to which he favoured his uninjured leg. Perhaps it was just the shadows, but she thought he had fleshed out a little. She felt inordinately pleased, as though she was in some way personally responsible for his progress.

'I'll go and make us both a cup of coffee,' he said quietly. 'I'm not pressuring you to confide in me, Rosy. I'm no father confessor, but something's bothering you.'

'What makes you think that?' she demanded, suddenly prickly with defensiveness.

He paused as he drew level with her, his shadow engulfing her, all at once making her feel frail and vulnerable.

'Too many anomalies; too many ends that don't tie up; too many shadows in your eyes.'

She thought about what he had said while he was in the kitchen, and wondered if she actually had the courage to confide in him. Not that confiding in him would solve her problem...but it might help her to get things in perspective, she recognised. He was a man who lived his life without any sexual relationships and was apparently both contented and fulfilled. She, on the other hand, was neither. She was a woman outwardly, but inwardly still very much a child.

By the time he came back she had made up her mind. Taking a deep breath, she said unevenly, 'I *would* like to talk to you, if I may.'

His eyes crinkled, and for the moment she tensed, thinking he was laughing at her, and then she realised that his smile was simply one of gentle reassurance.

As he handed her her coffee their fingers touched, and she realised that hers were cold with nervousness. There was something soothing about the brief, warm contact with his, and for a moment she wanted to cling on to him. Like a child clinging to security, she thought ironically as he moved away from her and went back to his seat in the shadows.

'I suppose the best thing to do would be for me to start at the beginning.'

'It generally is,' he agreed, mocking her gently.

'Well, you know about my upbringing...how isolated it was. I suppose really it started then, although at that stage I wasn't really aware of it. It was when I went to university...I got involved with someone there, a fellow undergraduate. Before that I'd never really given much thought to the way I was living my life, to how different it was from those of other girls of my age.' She moved uncomfortably in her seat, expressions chasing one another across her face, revealing far more than she herself realised.

Motionless in the shadows, Callum might almost not have been there, she recognised briefly. Looking up unsteadily, her hand trembling, she took a sip of her too hot coffee and then blew on it coolingly in a way she knew her great-aunt would have chided her for.

'So...this young man became your lover,' Callum said calmly. 'And...'

Rosy put down her coffee and denied urgently, 'No...Gareth and I were never lovers. That's the whole problem, Callum. I haven't *had* a lover,' she said tiredly. 'Of course, I couldn't hide my inexperience from Gareth. It turned him off completely. He was quite frank about it. He said he'd no desire to waste his time with a girl who was a virgin, not when there were so many around who were not...who knew exactly what to do to...to please him. I was stunned. It had never occurred to me...well, that something like that would happen.

'I suppose I'd imagined in some woolly-headed sort of way that I'd fall madly in love with someone and he with me and that we'd fall into bed, and that everything would be wonderful, and then I realised it wasn't going to be like that at all. I started refusing dates. I was terrified of someone else rejecting me as Gareth had...and my inexperience was so total that it wouldn't have taken them very long.'

'Was?' Callum questioned sharply.

She had almost forgotten he was there, and the sound of his voice made her focus on him. The light had gone completely now. He hadn't switched on the lamps, and only the firelight illuminated the room.

It was difficult for her to see his expression, and she frowned, searching the shadows and seeing only the outline of his face and the reflection of the fire-light on his glasses.

'Was and is,' she admitted bitterly. 'To have to admit to being totally inexperienced sexually at nineteen is bad enough. To have to make the same admission at twenty-five is virtually impossible. It isn't exactly something you can go out and enrol in a crash-course for,' she added bitterly. 'Oh, I know you probably find it hard to understand. You obviously find your life totally fulfilling, but I'm not sure if your kind of total celibacy is what I want. In fact, I know it isn't,' she admitted honestly. 'But how can I even begin to form a relationship with someone when all the time I'm terrified that the moment he touches me he's going to reject me?'

She sat dejectedly in her chair, suddenly running out of words, mortally afraid that she had said too much already. She was quite sure that really Callum had no desire at all to be burdened with the tacky emotionalism of her private problems and hang-ups.

As she looked at him, she realised he had moved a little and she could now see him more clearly. He looked oddly tense, and she wondered for a moment if he was in pain. She knew that his leg wound bothered him at times.

'Tell me something,' he asked her sombrely. 'If you hadn't thought—er—known about my celibacy... would you have told me any of this?'

It wasn't the question she had expected, and for a moment she was nonplussed, but then she shook her head and said wryly, 'No, I don't think so.'

He looked at her for what seemed like a long time, and then said abruptly, 'Well, in the good old days, I suppose the answer would have been to go out and find yourself a one-night stand you would never have to see again, but, given the prevailing risks of having sex with someone whose past history you don't know, that would hardly be a wise course of action.'

'No,' Rosy agreed brittly, and then added quickly, before she could lose her courage, 'and anyway, that wouldn't really do. It isn't just a matter of losing my virginity... it's the fact that I just don't have *any* kind of sexual experience...'

He was standing up, though she hadn't seen him do so.

He looked a little flushed, she realised, and wondered if she had embarrassed him. It was, after all, a rather personal subject to be discussing with a man she had known for less than a full week.

In other circumstances she might have eventually been able to confide in Bea, had she not been relatively sure that Bea might feel compelled to share her confidences with Elliott.

She *had* embarrassed him, she decided guiltily, watching the uncomfortable way in which Callum moved as he turned his back to her and asked, 'Er—not even the odd—er—teenage experimentation?'

The tips of his ears were burning dark red, she saw as she admitted, 'No... not even that. You see, when I was a teenager I rarely saw any other teenagers.'

She expected him to drop the subject, knowing that he was embarrassed by it, but to her surprise he pressed on determinedly. 'What about parties? Surely there must have been the usual games... Postman's knock, that sort of thing.'

'No,' Rosy told him sadly. 'I went to an all-girls' school, and my great-aunt never allowed me to go to any parties.'

He had turned round and was looking at her. His ears weren't red any more. He took off his glasses and rubbed his eyes tiredly. He had very thick black lashes that curled slightly, adding an unexpected softness to the thinness of his face.

He put his glasses back on and said, 'Rosy...'

But she wasn't listening to him; having come so far, she had a sudden fierce desire to abandon every last ounce of caution and reveal the appalling sum of her inadequacies.

'It's no good,' she told him. And, without her knowing it was going to happen, her mouth quivered unhappily and a tear rolled down her cheek. She sniffed hard, and swallowed the threatening sobs.

'I suppose you think I'm an absolute idiot,' she said weakly, trying to smile.

He muttered something she couldn't catch, but which sounded violent.

Later, when she had time to think logically about what had happened, she felt both appalled and embarrassed by her own behaviour. What on earth had possessed her to confide so deeply and intimately in Callum, whom she barely knew, things about herself she had previously only allowed herself to bring to light in her own mind, preferably in the privacy of her own bedroom where there was no one to question or comment on her inadequacies?

She went hot and then cold at the very idea of having to face Callum on Monday morning, cravenly wishing there was some way she could simply close her eyes and will the events of Friday evening to be erased from both their memories, and yet when she wasn't worrying about the fool she had made of herself she found that she was missing Callum, that time dragged ... that the company of William and the others, easy and undemanding though it was, was rather like living off candy-floss while craving a meal of bread and cheese.

Several times on Saturday she looked out of the narrow Victorian window of the terraced house, craving for the view from Callum's sitting-room, where the eye was stretched across rolling hills.

At least a dozen times she found herself idly wondering what Callum was doing, worrying about whether he had remembered to put on a warm jacket when he went outside, before taking herself severely to task, reminding herself that Callum was a grown man and that he had managed to survive very well without her and no doubt would go on surviving without her.

The Haydn concert, though enjoyable, failed to hold her attention as it ought to have done, and then on Sunday morning, while she and William were enjoying a late brunch, the others already having left the house, the telephone rang.

William answered it and came back to tell her rather tersely that it had been Bea, and that she and Elliott were coming to Oxford for a few days to have a short break from the children and do some shopping.

'They won't be staying here,' William told her, not looking at her. 'Elliott has booked them into an hotel.'

Rosy was tempted to tell him how he had misinterpreted what he had seen in Elliott's study, but one look at his frown warned her that he was unlikely to believe her.

Whereas before Bea's telephone call they had been chatting comfortably together, now he had withdrawn from her, and Rosy could see in his eyes suspicion and wariness.

She wondered a little enviously what it would be like to have brothers and sisters as closely protective of her as Bea's were. And then reminded herself rather sharply that it had been her impulsive longing for the close warmth of a family that had led to the mess she was in now in the first place.

It was almost ten days before Bea and Elliott's planned visit, but already, within hours of hearing about it, she was on edge and tense. Too late to regret now that she had not followed her first instinct to return to Northumberland.

Uncomfortable now in William's obviously disapproving presence, she escaped, with the excuse that she wanted to explore Oxford while the centre of the town was relatively quiet.

In the event, she did little more than wander past some of the ancient university buildings, before walking back to her car, painfully acknowledging that it was too late now to leave Oxford and go home.

Although she had only been working for him for a few days, it hadn't taken her long to realise how much Callum did need an assistant. Economics was not her field, but he had a way of simplifying even the most complicated financial intricacies so that they immediately became clear, and he had drawn for her a very graphic verbal picture of the world economics that had all played their part in Ethiopia's famine.

The pity of it was that, without a cessation of the civil war still being waged there, there was really little hope of the country and its people recovering enough to become self-sufficient in their pro- duction of food.

Economics were not simply graphs and columns of figures, he had told her with that slow, rare smile that could transform his face so much, and, watching him and listening to him, Rosy had begun to understand a little of what motivated him, of what drove him, in fact, to exhaust himself writing articles and preparing lectures when she suspected that by rights he ought to be doing nothing other than recuperating from his illness.

While he was prepared to answer as many ques- tions about Ethiopia's economic situation as she wanted to put to him, when it came to his injury and the fever which had struck him down he was far less forthcoming.

From the terse details he had given her, she had had to use her imagination to cobble together a true picture of what had happened.

His admission that he had had lassa fever had shocked her. Not because she was afraid for her own personal safety—she was sensible enough to realise that he couldn't be in any way contagious—but because of the appalling lack of proper medical care he had inadvertently betrayed in telling her the reason for his far too short hair.

It seemed impossible to believe that there were still parts of the world where hospitals were run under what seemed almost Dickensian conditions, and she shuddered a little as she drove back to the house, acknowledging that only a very tough human being could have survived such conditions.

Callum, tough? She thought of his tall, too thin body, his scholarly stoop, the glasses without which he seemed unable to see more than a few feet, and reflected that it was just as well that he had inner resources to make up for his lack of physical strength.

Oddly enough, on Sunday night she slept well. Her room at the top of the house was quiet and airy, and she didn't wake up until Chrissie knocked and popped her head round the door.

'I wasn't sure if you'd want waking up or nor, but it's gone eight...'

'It can't be!' Rosy protested, sitting up and grimacing as she saw the time. 'Thank goodness you woke me. I'm going to be late!'

She saw that Chrissie was staring at her and grimaced again.

'I suppose I look a wreck, do I?' she questioned the younger girl.

'Some wreck,' Chrissie responded enviously. 'You don't know how lucky you are to be naturally blonde. I wish my hair was like yours . . . so beautifully straight . . .'

Rosy gave her a wry grin. 'When I was at university I had it permed. The worst mistake I ever made. It looked like a frizz-ball. Straight hair's fine, but it has to be washed every day and cut regularly.'

'I'd still swap you,' Chrissie told her cheerfully. 'William says his sister and her husband are coming over for a visit. What's she like, his sister? He talks an awful lot about her . . .'

Chrissie was standing by the window with her back to her, but Rosy noticed that her shoulders were slightly tense. Chrissie was an extremely forthright young woman with very definite opinions and the experience of growing up alongside three brothers, and she treated her fellow housemates with a cheerful bossiness that Rosy quite envied, arguing passionately with them, treating them very much as Rosy suspected she did her brothers. A robust, bouncy girl, who looked and sounded sometimes as though sensitivity was an alien emotion to her. Rosy paused and studied her thoughtfully.

Only with William was her manner different . . . William's occasional sardonic comments drove her to retaliate like a spitting cat, and Rosy sighed for the foibles of her sex and its vulnerabilities.

'Bea's a darling,' she told her truthfully. 'Very warm and caring. She virtually brought William and Mirry up.'

'Yes, I know. According to William, she's everything the perfect wife and mother ought to be...devoting herself to her home and family.' Her chin jutted out slightly and she said belligerently, 'If and when *I* marry, I intend to carry on with my career. If I have children, I shall expect my husband to share their upbringing. I won't be a doormat.'

'Neither is Bea,' Rosy told her mildly, hiding her sympathy. She suspected she knew what was bugging the other girl.

'Bea is a very intelligent lady. She chose the way she lives, Chrissie. It wasn't chosen for her. After all, that's what it's supposed to be all about, isn't it...the right to choose for ourselves...the right for women to decide for themselves how they want to live their lives? Only, of course, no one is ever completely free. There are always obligations...responsibilities...which have to be juggled as best we can...'

Suddenly realising the time, Rosy broke off and grabbed her toilet-bag and clean underwear, calling over her shoulder, 'If you've got time, could you be a love and make me a cup of coffee? A strong cup of coffee.'

Half an hour later, driving down the narrow lane that led to Callum's cottage, Rosy felt the nervous tremors start to invade her stomach.

Every time she remembered the orgy of self-pity she had wallowed in in front of him, she wondered how on earth she was going to face him. He must be wondering if he had been mad to offer her a job, she thought wryly. An emotional, insecure woman eager to unburden her problems on to him must be the very last thing he wanted.

Inured against emotionalism himself, cloistered away from the kind of relationship problems that beset other people by virtue of the way he lived his life, he must surely be regretting inviting her to off-load hers on to him.

As the cottage came into view, she wondered idly if he had always lived the celibate, scholarly life he lived now, immersed in his work which was really more of a vocation ... shunning the turmoil of relationships based on physical and emotional attraction.

The sun came out as she parked her car, and as she got out and shut the door she noticed that the pansies which had been mere coloured buds sheathed in velvet green on Friday were now almost bursting open. She studied them, fascinated by the rich contrast of the bright, papery petals and the feathery green leaves, unaware that Callum had come out of the cottage until she saw his shadow and looked up to see him standing beside her.

She blushed a little. She couldn't help it, wishing desperately that she had not given in to that stupid urge to confide in him. Not so much in *him*, she recognised wryly, looking away from him but unable to capture her earlier absorption in the pansies. What had happened on Friday evening had been the cloudburst effect of too many months of bottled-up strain and depression following her great-aunt's death, brought to a head by the shock and pain of realising how horribly Mirry and William and even Elliott himself had misread her feelings. That pain...that hurt...that feeling of being rejected by the only family she had left had reactivated that old pain of her student days, forcing it to the forefront of her mind.

She had unburdened herself to Callum simply because he'd had the misfortune to be there. She sighed a little, reflecting that she now had something far more pressing to worry about.

How on earth was she going to be able to behave naturally with Bea and Elliott when they arrived, especially with William looking on suspiciously, gauging her every word and movement?

And what if...horror of horrors...Elliott had actually confided to Bea that he suspected her of developing a crush on him? She went white at the thought. She liked Bea so much, and would hate the other woman to think that. It would demean her completely in Bea's eyes, and there could never be the same warmth and trust between them again, no matter that Elliott was quite wrong.

'They're simply pansies...rather splendid, but not so very out of the ordinary...'

Callum's quiet words checked her thoughts. She looked at him without thinking, her eyes widening a little as she realised he had taken off his glasses and was cleaning them, and she could actually see the colour of his eyes. They were the most extra-ordinary sea-green, and she stared at them, blinking a little at the unexpectedness of them. He was still cleaning his glasses, his movements careful and de-

liberate. The sun went behind a cloud, and Rosy
remembered how much Callum felt the cold. She
reached out and touched his arm lightly, wincing a
little in compassion as she felt the hardness of the
bone so clearly through his skin. He made no reference at all to Friday evening, for which she was
profoundly grateful, and within half an hour of her
arrival they were so deeply immersed in work that
she completely forgot her self-consciousness.

It was only over lunch, a pasta dish made by
Callum, who had surprised her a little by being such
a good cook—she had expected for some reason
that he would have a scholarly lack of concern for
food and regular meals—that she started worrying
again about Bea and Elliott's visit. She would need
to ask Callum for some time off. If Bea was going
shopping, she would surely expect Rosy to go with
her.

She asked him a little apologetically, feeling guilty
about asking for time off so early in their working
relationship, explaining what had happened.

'You don't sound very happy about their visit,'
he commented, pouring them both a second cup of
coffee from the jug he had made.

'I'm not,' she admitted, nursing the welcome
warmth of the full cup between her hands. 'It won't
be easy facing Elliott, knowing that he thinks I'm
half-way to falling in love with him.'

'And are you?'

The question surprised her, making her frown at
him and put down her coffee.

'I've already explained to you, Elliott is my
cousin . . . the only family I have left. No, I'm not

in love with him,' she told him shortly. 'I can understand William and Mirry—just about—but Elliott... And I suppose, once Mirry finds out, she'll be pushing William even harder to get me matched up with someone and safely out of the way. I'm beginning to think I should have gone straight back to Northumberland as I'd originally intended. It would have been the best solution.'

'Not necessarily.'

The calm words caught her attention. She looked at Callum queryingly, but he didn't look back at her. He appeared to be concentrating on buttering a cheese biscuit, a task which was apparently extremely demanding.

'There *is* an alternative.'

'Such as?' Rosy asked him ungraciously.

'I presume from all that you've told me that the production of an established lover would be sufficient to calm the turbulent familial waters,' he offered pedantically.

'Yes, it would,' Rosy agreed tightly. 'Were such a thing possible, and if you're thinking of suggesting I make up a fictitious lover, I don't think that would work. Bea is very much the family type and would be bound to want to meet him. Elliott too, I suspect, although for a different motive. Elliott can be extremely ruthless if he feels the occasion demands it, and I suspect he's determined to make me fully aware that it's Bea he loves and that my supposed crush doesn't stand a chance of ever being anything more than sheer fantasy, so to simply tell them that I'm involved with someone else just wouldn't work. Elliott would expect me to produce him, and we both know I can't do that . . .'

There was a small silence, and then Callum pushed his plate aside and said quietly, 'We could if we were to pretend that I'm your lover.'

Rosy was too stunned to say or do anything other than simply gape at him, her eyes rounding in astonishment.

'You? But, Callum . . .' She thought of Elliott's reaction to such an announcement. He would take one look at Callum and . . . She swallowed hard, knowing that there was no way she could tell Callum just what Elliott's reaction would be. To do so would be cruelly hurtful to a man who was, after all, only trying to help her; to draw attention to the obvious physical differences between Elliott and the man sitting next to her, to highlight the fact that Elliott was an extremely virile and attractively male man, while Callum . . . She drew a shaky breath. She just couldn't do it.

It was a long time before she felt sufficiently in control of her emotions to lift her head and look directly at him, and she prayed that he wouldn't be able to read what was in her mind.

She didn't want to hurt him, but the thought of anyone believing that a woman who was supposed to be in love with Elliott would turn from him to Callum was just so painfully impossible.

He was obviously waiting for her to make some additional comment, but what could she say?

She cleared her throat.

'Callum, it's unbelievably kind of you, but are you sure you really mean it?'

Tears of gratitude stung her throat. It no longer mattered that no one would see Callum as sexual competition for Elliott—what mattered was the true friendship behind the offer.

'Of course I mean it,' he replied calmly. 'And what's more, you could make it seem even more real. You could move in here—with me.'

CHAPTER FIVE

'MOVE in? Here? With you?' Rosy stared at Callum in disbelief. 'But . . .'

'It's the most logical thing to do,' he pointed out to her, apparently oblivious to her shock. 'I was thinking about it over the weekend. It takes you almost an hour to drive out here and then an hour to drive back. We're getting very close to the summer recess when Oxford will be packed with tourists, and you'll find the traffic very bad. Add to that the fact that when the long vacation does start you'd probably find yourself living alone, since your cousin and his friends will most probably migrate either to their parental homes or to holiday jobs.

'There's more than enough room for you here and, from a purely selfish point of view, it would suit me admirably to have you here on hand, so to speak. Quite often in the evening I find myself suddenly thinking of some notes I'd like to make and, as you've probably noticed, I don't find it as easy to use the dictaphone as I do to dictate direct to you.'

That much was true. Rosy had noticed that he didn't like the dictaphone, and that when he did use it his dictation was considerably less fluent.

'If you're worried that because you're living here I'll expect you to take over the domestic chores, I assure you that you needn't be. Were your circumstances different...if you were involved in an—er—intimate relationship, I must admit I wouldn't be making this suggestion.' He gave her a small smile. 'It's irrational of me, I know, given the fact that I've chosen my—er—celibate life-style quite freely, but I suspect there would be a certain awkwardness in our relationship were you to want to have your lover staying here overnight; but since that's hardly likely to apply... From your point of view,' he continued, not waiting for her to respond, 'the fact that you were living with me, so to speak, would be bound to add a great degree of weight to the fiction that you and I are lovers.'

Rosy heard his latter comment, but made no response to it, her face still burning from the mental images Callum had conjured up by his earlier statement. The thought of her living under Callum's roof and casually inviting some other man into her house to share her bed made her shiver with a distaste she couldn't explain.

'You're not worried that if you moved in here I might be tempted to take advantage of the situation, are you, Rosy?' Callum asked her quietly.

She was so engrossed in her own thoughts that it took several seconds for the quiet words to penetrate. When they did, her face burned scarlet. She stared at him as though she couldn't believe what she was hearing, and almost stammered, 'Of course not.'

'Good,' he murmured, apparently unaware of her embarrassment. 'Because when I suggested you move in here I wasn't suggesting that we sleep together.'

He wasn't looking at her, for which Rosy was heartily grateful. In fact, he seemed to have drifted off into some world of his own, because he continued ruminatively, more to himself than her, as though he was engaged on working out some abstract calculation rather than dealing with an emotional human problem. 'Of course, if I had a housekeeper or a daily coming in it might have perhaps been necessary to consider it, in order to preserve the fiction of our relationship as lovers, but, since I don't, it would hardly seem likely that your cousin and his family are likely to discover the truth. The simple announcement that we are living together should be sufficient, wouldn't you say, backed up perhaps by dinner one evening during their visit...?'

Rosy was practically speechless, but he seemed unaware of it, or of the reason for her silence. Giving her a preoccupied smile, he announced, 'Excellent, so that's all settled. I'll let you choose your own room, although you might prefer the one at the far end, it's closest to the second bathroom, and I think it might be as well if I come back with you this evening when you go back to Oxford to collect your stuff. It won't do any harm to get in a bit of practice at playing our new roles.'

Rosy glanced wildly at him, and then closed her eyes in mental supplication to whatever fates had decided to meddle so mischievously and unwantedly in her life.

*   *   *

They spent the rest of the afternoon working, Callum rattling off dictation at a speed that made it impossible for her to do anything other than fight to keep pace with him.

She was an intelligent girl, and suspected that he was deliberately keeping her too busy to spend any time pursuing second thoughts about the wisdom of what they were doing. Since, despite what he had said to her about the convenience of having her 'living in' while she worked for him, the major benefits in them pretending to be lovers could only be hers, she acknowledged that he had an awareness of other people's emotions and a compassion for them that was very rare.

How many other men would have taken the trouble to find out what was worrying her, and then to act so promptly and so selflessly in finding a solution? Very, very few, and as she looked at his dark head as he bent over some notes he was dictating to her Rosy felt an unfamiliar welling of tenderness inside her.

His hair was just growing long enough to flop down over his forehead, and he pushed it out of the way as he bent over his work. It was very thick and fine, and shone with a healthy gleam that seemed to cruelly underline his wasted flesh.

She was beginning to recognise the early signs of his tiredness now: the tension that hardened his jaw when he wanted to go on working but knew that he should rest; the way he removed his glasses and rubbed his eyes as though they were sore; the slight thickening and slowing of his voice; and now, as she saw them and mentally calculated how long it would be before he gave in and admitted that he needed to rest, she took advantage of a break in his concentration to get up and say calmly, 'I'll go and make us both a drink, shall I?'

Before he put his glasses back on, she saw the gleam in his eyes.

'You're not by any chance trying to mother me, are you Rosy?'

Rosy suspected that he knew the answer as well as she did, but she said calmly, 'You said yourself that your doctor said you weren't to push yourself too hard. I believe it's normal practice in an office environment to stop for a drink some time during the afternoon.'

She was remembering him telling her that he loathed being fussed over, and for some reason she wasn't at all sure she really understood herself she recognised that she was enjoying working for him . . . that it stretched her mind in a way she was only just beginning to realise she had missed during the long months of looking after her aunt, and that she wanted to keep her temporary job with him.

'Anyway,' she told him calmly, '*I'm* ready for a cup of coffee, even if you aren't.'

The half-derisory look he gave her as she whisked herself out of the room made her very conscious of how formidable a person he must have been before his illness struck him down. In the kitchen, making the coffee, she frowned a little over that acknowledgement, a little perturbed by the knowledge without being able to say why.

There was certainly nothing about Callum that threatened her sexually. She felt no apprehension when he looked at her, no frantic desire to protect and conceal herself as she did with other men.

And that, surely, was as much because he already knew the truth about her as it was because of his own aesthetic, celibate attitude towards her?

Callum could become the close friend she had never had, she reflected as she filled two mugs with coffee...the person she could turn to in times of need or stress, the person with whom she could be honest and open about her feelings and fears, knowing that she would not be derided or mocked for them, knowing that he would understand.

When she opened the study door he was leaning back in his chair with his eyes closed. At first she thought he was asleep, but the moment she walked into the room his eyes opened and focused on her, his pupils dark and brilliant.

'I'll just finish this section, and then we'll go and collect your stuff.'

'There's really no need to come with me,' Rosy told him, thinking it would probably be easier if she made the announcement on her own, but Callum shook his head, and said with that odd, unsuspected firmness she was beginning to recognise,

'I'm coming.' He saw the uncertainty in her face and put down his papers, getting up with the awkwardness that always seemed to grip him when he had been sitting down for a long period. As she had known he would do, he massaged his injured thigh, his fingers digging into the muscle, as he limped over to the window, and stood there with his back to her, his voice slightly muffled as he said curtly, 'Put yourself in William's place. What would you think of a lover who allows the woman in his life to make the announcement of their joint decision to live together on her own? He'll expect me to be with you.'

After that, there was nothing further that Rosy could say. As she bent her head over her notebook, she wondered a little wryly if anyone had ever won an argument with Callum. He was so calmly, so gently logical—so immovable, she recognised wryly.

At five-thirty Callum announced that they had done enough and that it was time they left for Oxford. Rosy had learned to drive during her last year at school and, after much discussion and consideration, and having checked first with the driving school, Aunt Maud had bought her her first car for her eighteenth birthday. Having a car had made life easier for both of them, but those early years of having as a passenger an irascible and rather timid elderly lady had given Rosy an awareness of the emotional and physical comforts of her passengers which she had never lost.

Callum, though, like William, turned out to be one of those rare males who neither braced himself nor grimaced, nor made muttered comments about the ability of female drivers, and seemed quite content to leave Rosy in complete charge of their transportation. The only comment he did make was that it might perhaps have been wiser for them to have travelled to Oxford in his Mercedes, because this would have given them more boot space for Rosy's possessions on the return journey.

However, Rosy told him that, since her original visit to Elliott and Bea had only been going to be a brief one, all she had with her were a couple of medium-sized suitcases.

Out of the corner of her eye she saw his eyebrows rise a little as she delivered this comment, but all he said as he leaned back in his seat and closed his eyes was, 'Rosy, the more I get to know about you, the more I am convinced that you are a paragon among your sex.'

Rosy could have informed him that she had been hard put to it to fill those two suitcases for her visit. Great-Aunt Maud had been a thrifty character and, even though Rosy had been left very comfortably off by her parents' and grandparents' death, Maud had never encouraged her to spend money wastefully. Great-Aunt Maud was of the generation that considered that a good suit should last a woman for at least ten years, and it had only been with the utmost difficulty that Rosy had allowed Great-Aunt Maud to agree that she should buy herself a pair of jeans. Even then she had been banned from wearing them in the cottage.

Consequently Rosy had learned as a teenager to manage with a very slender wardrobe indeed, a habit which she still found hard to break, even though she loved new clothes. It was difficult for her to go out and indulge herself in a spending spree without imagining Aunt Maud's critical and warning voice in her ear.

She had bought new clothes for her visit to Elliott and Bea. Nothing outrageously fashionable, just simple and elegant things which she had bought at

Jaeger, for once managing to throw off a little of the caution Aunt Maud had instilled in her, and then feeling shakily appalled by the amount of money she had spent when she had got her purchases home.

The clothes suited her slender blonde elegance, and she knew that she would not have felt at ease with a wardrobe of up-to-the-minute, extravagantly outrageous fashionable items. Even so, she couldn't entirely repress the small stab of feminine annoyance at Callum's comment, which caused her to depress the accelerator just a little harder than she had been doing, so that without her being aware of it Callum opened his eyes and watched her thoughtfully for a few seconds.

After more than a week Rosy was now becoming familiar with the layout of Oxford's main streets, and she deftly manoeuvred her car so that they avoided the main bulk of the rush-hour traffic.

'I don't know how many of the others will be in,' she warned him as she turned into the road that led to the house. 'William should be there. It's his turn to make the evening meal tonight.' And then she went on to explain the rota with which the household was organised.

'Well, let's hope young William doesn't object too forcefully to our announcement.'

'He's far more likely to fall on your neck with cries of gratitude,' Rosy told him wryly, adding as she stopped the car, 'Oh, and perhaps I should warn you that he's extremely impressed by the fact that I'm working for you. You're something of a hero to him academically.'

She locked the car and waited for Callum to join her on the pavement. They walked up the front path together, Rosy using her key to let them in to the long, narrow hallway. The sound of their arrival drew William from the kitchen. He saw Rosy and greeted her absently, quite obviously nonplussed when he realised Callum was standing behind her.

Rosy introduced them, and was just about to suggest making them all a cup of tea when, to her astonishment, Callum put his arm very firmly round her waist, bridging the small gap between them so that her hip rested against the hardness of his thigh. The sensation of feeling the bones so clearly through the thick fabric of his jeans filled her with such a compassionate awareness of his physical fragility that for a moment she forgot her shock at the unexpected intimacy of his gesture and simply stood there looking up at him, unaware of the easily readable play of emotions across her face.

'Well, darling, shall I tell William our news, while you pop upstairs and collect your stuff?' The question, asked in a voice whose caressing quality made her eyes widen a little, caused her to stare at him, nonplussed. For some reason his assumption of authority had surprised her. Quite how she had expected they would break the news to William, she wasn't really sure. All she did know was that the sensation of Callum's arm round her waist, and the easy way in which he was discussing their proposed relationship, was making her feel as dithery and self-conscious as she had been as a shy and introverted teenager.

William was gaping slightly at both of them, quite obviously as shocked by Callum's announcement as she had been herself, and then he started to frown, the mild blue eyes behind his glasses betraying his concern, which Rosy found wholly unexpected, and rather touching. A ridiculous lump of emotional response lodged in her throat as she watched William almost physically squaring his shoulders, suddenly very much the protective male as he invited Callum into the sitting-room.

Although the hallway wasn't very wide, Callum didn't make any move to release her, and so Rosy found herself being very gently but firmly propelled towards the sitting-room door, Callum's hand resting now on her hip, so that as they followed William into the room they presented the image of a physically united couple.

William cleared his throat and, avoiding looking directly at her, said to Callum, 'I'm sorry, I don't think I understand.'

Callum's smile could have disarmed a hostile army, Rosy reflected, studying it.

'It's quite simple, really,' Callum told him easily. 'Rosy and I have fallen in love and I have persuaded her that I'll recuperate much faster with her on hand to take charge of me.' As Rosy looked at him, gaping slightly, astounded by the wealth of sensual imagery which he had managed to inject into the softly spoken words, he looked back at her, smiling at her in a way that made her unprepared body tense with shock.

She had to blink to dispel the vision of that promising, desirous look, totally bemused by

Callum's ability to project such an image. She looked from him to William, and discovered that the latter was looking both embarrassed and concerned.

'How about a cup of tea,' Callum suggested, 'while Rosy goes and packs?'

Acknowledging mentally that both of them had been given their instructions, Rosy started to move away from them and then found that she couldn't. She looked down uncertainly to where his hand rested on her hip. He wasn't exerting any particular kind of pressure, and yet somehow he had managed to constrain her. She looked back to him, puzzled by this behaviour, opening her mouth to remind him that she was supposed to be packing her clothes.

'Don't be too long, will you, darling?' The dark head bent towards her, the words a husky whisper, infused with an open sexual need that made her stare at him in disbelief. His body shielded her from William, his hands turning her into his body; his mouth against her ear, he whispered quietly, 'It's all right. It's all part of the act,' and then he was releasing her, turning her gently in the direction of the open door.

Half-way upstairs, Rosy discovered that she was breathing rather heavily and that her pulse was racing at an erratic rate. She wasn't sure if her shock had been caused by the unexpectedness of Callum's touch or his astounding ability to project such a powerfully believable image of a man deep in the throes of desire. Hardly aware of what she was doing, she opened the wardrobe in her bedroom and pulled out her suitcases, hurriedly filling them with her clothes.

Great-Aunt Maud's teaching was too engrained to allow her to simply stuff things into the cases, and so automatically she folded and packed, tensing when her bedroom door opened unexpectedly and William came in. He was frowning, his face both concerned and embarrassed.

'Rosy, are you sure this is wise?' he blurted out without preamble. 'I mean...well, you've only known him barely a week,' he added in an embarrassed mutter as she stopped what she was doing and stared across the room at him.

'I thought you liked him,' she said quietly, when she had got over the shock of realising that William was genuinely concerned for her.

He grimaced slightly and muttered under his breath, 'He's the best economics lecturer there is, but that doesn't mean——' He broke off, his ears going red, and said urgently, 'Rosy, wait until Bea and Elliott are here before you make any decision.'

His concern for her had touched her, but the moment he mentioned Elliott's name her determination hardened.

'This is my decision, not theirs,' she told him firmly, and then softened a little when she saw the unhappiness in his eyes. 'William, I'm twenty-five years old,' she reminded him, 'and since my aunt's death I've become used to making my own decisions.'

'Yes,' he agreed, and then, a little to her surprise, continued with dogged intentness, 'I still think you should wait, though. You've only known him a week.' He scowled darkly, and then added in embarrassment, 'You could stay here and still go out with him, and then, when you get engaged...'

'Engaged?' Rosy stared at him, openly astonished.

His scowl deepened, and an expression she had never expected to see on the face of such a mild-tempered young man darkened his eyes surprisingly. 'He is going to marry you, isn't he?' he demanded.

Rosy had no idea what to say. It was a question she was totally unprepared for. Had it been her Great-Aunt Maud she was facing, then she might have expected such an inquisition, but from William, child of a generation who accepted as by right the wisdom of experiencing more than one sexual partner before making a commitment that was supposed to last for life...that William should stand there and glower at her like a Victorian parent lecturing a daughter on the dangers of allowing a man too many favours was something so unexpected that she couldn't think of a single response she could make. And William drew his own conclusions from her silence, his frustration and despair intensifying.

As he stood in the doorway for one moment, Rosy wondered if he was going to attempt to physically prevent her from rejoining Callum, and then she reminded herself that she was twenty-five years old and William not yet twenty-two, and moreover that his only relationship with her was that of a very distant cousinship, and then only by marriage. She said firmly, 'It's very thoughtful of you to be so concerned on my behalf, William, but I do assure you that I know exactly what I'm doing,' and then, seeing the indecision in his face, she softened and added, 'I'm doing the right thing, William, I promise you that.'

As she fastened her suitcase and headed for the door, he took it from her and said glumly, under his breath, 'Let's hope Elliott agrees with you.'

Smiling easily at him, and hiding her own inner feelings, Rosy said calmly but with very firm emphasis, 'William, Elliott has as little authority to dictate to me how I live my life as you do.' And then, very determinedly, she walked downstairs and back into the sitting-room.

When she got back into the sitting-room, Callum was sitting on the settee, holding a sheaf of hand-written papers in his hand. William was right behind her, and it was to him Callum spoke and not Rosy herself, saying approvingly, 'That's an interesting theory you're expounding in this piece, William.'

But when Rosy turned round to look at him, she saw that, although William was very obviously gratified by his praise, he was also still very wary, regarding them both with frowning uncertainty.

Rosy wouldn't let Callum carry her bags out to the car. They weren't particularly heavy, but she had noticed the small, betraying movement that meant that his leg was bothering him, and she could see that he was beginning to get tired.

All three of them went to the front door together, and as Rosy opened it William said almost desperately, 'Look, why don't you stay here, at least until Bea and Elliott arrive?'

Before Rosy could make any response, Callum shook his head and said calmly but firmly, 'I want Rosy with me,' and then, before Rosy herself could say a word, he was guiding her back towards the car, his quiet, 'Would you prefer me to drive?' as she unlocked the door making her focus on him and smile a little wryly.

'No, it's OK. I think I'll be all right,' she told him, adding honestly, 'I hadn't expected William to make such a fuss, but at least he seems to have accepted it now.'

'Mm...' Callum agreed non-committally, getting into the passenger seat when she had opened the door. It amazed Rosy that William had believed that they were lovers so easily, but he had seemed far more concerned with preventing her from moving in with Callum than questioning the truth about their relationship, and she acknowledged that if Callum hadn't been with her she might have found it very difficult to prevent herself from telling him the truth.

'What did he say to you when you were upstairs?' Callum asked her once they were clear of the town centre.

Rosy shot him a surprised look, wondering how he knew William had followed her up there. He gave her an odd smile and said softly, 'It stands to reason. He has a very highly developed sense of responsibility, and you are in his charge, so to speak.'

Rosy raised her eyebrows ready to point out she was an independent single woman and no one's responsibility, least of all a twenty-one-year-old boy who was only related to her by marriage.

Callum shook his head and said firmly, 'No, I'm not being a chauvinist. I'm simply telling you how William feels. By the way, while you were upstairs I told him we'd be getting in touch to arrange to go out to dinner with your cousin and his wife once they arrive in Oxford.'

'Poor William,' said Rosy softly. 'I think he was torn between his admiration for you and his disapproval of the fact that I'm moving in with you. He told me the first time I mentioned meeting you that you were a very private person, and I suspect this relationship of ours doesn't fit in with his preconceived ideas about you.'

'Wrong,' Callum told her crisply. 'It's not me he's worried about, but you.'

'I don't see why he should be,' Rosy answered him a touch acerbically. 'After all, it's exactly what he wanted.'

They were almost half-way back to Callum's cottage now. The adrenalin-fuelled apprehension which had carried her through the interview with William and then out into her car in a state of righteous indignation that a mere twenty-one-year-old should take it upon himself to question her judgement had now gone, leaving her feeling oddly flat and not a little uncertain that she had made the wrong decision.

The truth was, she acknowledged silently, Callum had acted so decisively, putting his suggestion into practice so immediately after its initial inception, that she hadn't really had time to think about what she was doing, and yet, after all, what was there to feel apprehensive about? With Callum established as her lover, and that fiction backed up by the fact that she was living with him, there was now no need for her to feel apprehensive about Bea and Elliott's visit. No need for her to worry any more about those direct, assessing looks which Elliott used to peer deep into people's souls; no need to worry that Bea, whom she already loved so much, would begin to misinterpret her feelings as Elliott, William and Mirry had done, and start looking at her with doubt instead of affection.

She ought to be giving praise instead of feeling apprehensive. She had a job which she already loved, even if it was only a temporary one. She had found a family that she had never known existed. She had discovered a new purpose in life and a new energy to go with it. Instead of worrying herself into a state of miserable uncertainty, she ought to be looking forward to the future, a future when she should surely be able to laugh with Bea and Elliott about this fictitious relationship of hers with Callum.

'It's not too late to turn back, you know,' Callum told her quietly.

His percipience surprised her, although she admitted there was no reason why it should do and every reason why it shouldn't because he had already shown her how very intuitive he was about people's feelings, especially, it seemed, her own.

'You could always tell William that you've changed your mind and you're taking his advice.'

He sounded so calmly unconcerned that she immediately berated herself for her stupidity.

'No. I'm not changing my mind,' she told him firmly, and then added uncertainly, 'Unless, of course, you...'

'On the contrary,' he assured her easily. 'I'm looking forward to having a live-in secretary at my disposal. I've got one hell of a lot of work to get through between now and the end of the summer.'

In the small Victorian house, William was pacing the sitting-room floor while Chrissie stared belligerently at him.

'What do you mean, you should have stopped her?' she demanded militantly. 'She's a grown woman, William.'

He ignored her, muttering under his breath. 'Heaven knows what Elliott's going to say. I knew I should never have listened to Mirry.'

Chrissie's ears pricked up a little at this mention of his sister's name. William didn't talk a lot about his family, but the odd snatches of information he revealed fascinated her. They had known one another just under a year. Chrissie was two years younger than William, a bright, intelligent girl used to the bossiness of three older brothers and more than capable of holding her own against any macho dominance.

'I don't know what you're making such a fuss about,' she told him scornfully. 'After all, it isn't exactly as though this is the eighteen-nineties and she's gone off with a potential white slave-trader, is it?'

William's ears went red, a sure sign that he was both irritated and embarrassed, but he pressed on doggedly, 'She's only known him a week.'

'So what?' Chrissie derided. 'People fall in love in seconds. Look, if you're that worried,' she told him, 'you can always go out there and see them to check that everything's all right.'

'I don't have a car,' William pointed out glumly.

Chrissie smiled at him, batting long eyelashes.

'No, but I do,' she told him sweetly. 'It's on loan from my cousin.'

William gave her a preoccupied glower. He was wondering what on earth he was going to say to Elliott when the latter arrived in Oxford. He had a depressing feeling that Elliott wasn't going to be very pleased to discover that Rosy had moved in with Callum.

CHAPTER SIX

'WE MAY as well take this straight upstairs,' Callum announced as he lifted Rosy's cases out of the car, picking them up with an ease that surprised her. For all his frailty, he must be surprisingly strong. She gave him a doubtful look as she watched him walk towards the front door, and then hurried after him.

'Keys are in my jeans pocket,' he told her. 'Fish them out for me, will you?'

Obediently Rosy slid her hand into the right-hand pocket of his jeans, and then, discovering that it was deeper than she had expected, had to thrust her hand down deeper inside the worn denim fabric until her fingers found the small bunch of keys.

With her hand closed round them, it wasn't as easy to withdraw it from his pocket as she had expected, and an embarrassed flush of colour stained her skin as she felt the hard press of bone beneath the fabric.

Surely it was an oddly intimate suggestion from a man as celibate as Callum, and one that could have been more expected from a man more used to easy proximity with her sex than she had assumed Callum to be? But he moved awkwardly, reminding her that it must be tiring for him standing with her cases while he waited for her to unlock the door, so she removed her hand and the keys and, when he told her which was the right one, she used it to let them both in.

'I've got a spare set somewhere; I must find them for you,' he murmured as they went inside. 'I'm afraid you'll have to make up a bed for yourself, but you'll find plenty of clean linen, towels et cetera in the airing cupboard in the second bathroom. Oh, and by the way, if you don't mind, I'd like to give you some more dictation this evening. I have to go to London tomorrow to see the specialist. I'll probably be gone all day, so you'll have plenty of time to type it up. You'll want time off while your cousins are in Oxford.'

He had climbed the stairs with her cases without seeming the least bit tired, and Rosy followed him as he led the way to the end bedroom.

'I thought this one,' he told her, pushing open the door. 'But if you'd prefer one of the others...'

'No, this one is fine,' Rosy assured him.

It was a pretty room with marvellous views over the hills, and had the advantage of being right next door to the second bathroom which he had already told her she would have for her own exclusive use.

'Right, well, while you're unpacking, I'd better do something about dinner. Salmon suit you? I think we've got some salmon steaks in the freezer.'

'Lovely,' Rosy told him mechanically. As he put down her cases, the fabric of his jeans pulled taut against his hips. An unfamiliar heat burned her skin and her fingertips tingled disturbingly.

'Something wrong?' asked Callum as he straightened up. She shook her head, focusing on his face and wondering what on earth was wrong with her. She tried to speak, and found that her throat had become very dry.

'The specialist,' she said at last, 'what will he——?'

'It's just a routine check-up,' Callum interrupted her curtly. 'The bullet damaged a muscle, and there's a bit of a problem with it knitting together properly.'

'Probably because you don't rest it often enough,' said Rosy, recovering her composure, her expression slightly severe.

'Very likely,' he agreed blandly, but there was a warning glint in his eyes, and Rosy remembered that he had warned her he didn't want to be fussed over, so she turned away from him and went over to her suitcases, saying calmly, 'Salmon sounds fine for dinner. If I've got any time left over tomorrow while you're away, I could draw up a rota so that we can share the responsibility for making the meals.' And then she realised that she might be taking too much for granted and that Callum might prefer to eat alone, and so she paused and looked at him uncertainly and added, 'That is, of course, if you want us to eat together.'

'I'm not a misogynist, Rosy,' he told her wryly. 'And I enjoy intelligent, informed conversation over the dinner-table just as much as the next man. Of course I want us to eat together, although I'd better warn you that I do tend to be a touch surly first thing in the morning.'

Rosy stared at him. Compliments were the last thing she expected to receive from Callum, and she blinked a little, both flattered and a little uncertain.

The calm familiarity with which he had compli-
mented her spoke of a man long at ease with the
female sex, and yet by his very life-style she had
assumed that Callum, like herself, would be rather
more uncertain and wary of any intimacy with the
opposite sex.

After he had gone downstairs, leaving her to
unpack, she decided that his celibacy must be a
more recent development than she had previously
supposed, and wondered if it dated from before or
after his time in Ethiopia. It struck her as she made
up her bed that Callum knew far more about her
than she did about him. He was thirty-four years
old, and before coming to Oxford had apparently
lectured at St Andrews. William had described him
as a man who liked his privacy, and Rosy wondered
again if his celibacy had been freely chosen or
perhaps forced upon him by circumstances such as
being rejected by a woman following his illness.

Reminding herself that if Callum wanted to work
during the evening he wouldn't appreciate her
mooning about up here wasting time, she finished
making her bed and then hurried downstairs.

Callum was in the kitchen.

'Good timing,' he told her, smiling at her. 'The
salmon won't be long. I thought we'd eat in here,
if that's all right by you?'

The kitchen was a spacious, comfortable room,
and this wouldn't be the first time she had shared
a meal with Callum, so why did she suddenly feel
this almost claustrophobic awareness of Callum as
a man?

'Could you do the table?' Callum asked her over his shoulder, and Rosy hurried gratefully to the dresser where the china and cutlery were kept, glad of something to do which would take her mind off the far too introspective thoughts. It was natural that she should feel a little awkwardness, she told herself reassuringly as she laid two places at the plain, scrubbed table.

She and Callum were, after all, in many ways still strangers, and, even though she had been drawn to him right from the moment they met, there were bound to be moments of awkwardness and unease. After all, she reminded herself a little wryly, he *was* the first man she had lived with.

The thought made her smile, and, unaware that Callum was watching her, she was startled when he said softly, 'That's better.'

Her face, far too expressive ever to conceal her feelings, mirrored her confusion and guilt.

'Stop worrying,' he chided her gently. 'Everything's going to be fine.'

His calm assurance steadied her. She took a deep breath and said shakily, 'I can't think why on earth you're doing this for me.'

'I've told you,' he answered her, turning away from her to rescue the boiling potatoes, 'having a live-in secretary is going to prove very convenient. How long did you say it was before your cousin arrives in Oxford?' he asked her thoughtfully, as he drained the potatoes and put them on two warmed plates.

'Another eight or nine days, I think.'

'Mm...good. That gives us time to polish up our act a bit...'

'Polish up our act?' Rosy repeated uncertainly, her nose twitching appreciatively as he opened the oven and removed the succulent salmon steaks.

'Mm.' He was concentrating on manoeuvring the salmon on to their plates and replied rather absently, 'I suspect your cousin isn't going to be quite as easy to fool as William. Don't worry, though, between us we'll be more than a match for him. I've done green beans and carrots for veg. Is that OK?'

'Fine,' Rosy assured him, surprised to discover how hungry she felt.

The meal tasted every bit as good as it looked.

Economics wasn't a subject which had ever interested her particularly before she met Callum, but he had opened her eyes to its wide impact outside the sterile and dull world of written facts and collated information, so that she was beginning to grasp how the global economic situation affected different countries.

'So it isn't merely from philanthropic impulse that the wealthy western countries give aid to the poorer ones,' she had said to Callum several days earlier when he had been explaining to her the reasons behind his visit to Ethiopia. Since then she had discovered a compulsive fascination for this hitherto unknown world, and over dinner she and Callum discussed the likely impact of a United States decision to freeze funds deposited in American banks belonging to certain South

American states, as a way of controlling the activities of a government the Americans disliked because of its extreme left-wing political views.

From there they went on to discuss the effectiveness of certain economic sanctions against countries and governments, and when Callum eventually got up to make the coffee Rosy was amazed to discover how long they had been talking.

He must make a good lecturer, she reflected, watching him, his movements slightly awkward, as they always were whenever he had been sitting for some time. She was not surprised that William wanted to include Callum's lectures in his course, and then she remembered guiltily that Callum had wanted to spend the evening working, so she got up quickly from the table, gathering up their plates and cutlery and stacking them efficiently in the dishwasher.

'Where's the fire?' Callum teased her as he made the coffee.

'I've just remembered that you wanted to work this evening,' Rosy told him. 'We could take our coffee straight into the study,' she suggested earnestly, automatically loading the rest of the washing-up into the machine and then closing the door. She was standing right next to Callum, and as she pressed the dishwasher door closed with her hip she realised how very tall he was when he stood straight without stooping.

He gave her an amused smile, his eyes crinkling at the corners.

'All right, slave-driver. I don't know.' He sighed theatrically as he turned away from her to pour the coffee into their mugs. 'The lengths some people will go to avoid my conversation...'

Just in time Rosy realised that he was teasing her, and taking her mug from him, she said severely, 'Stop fishing.'

It was amazing, Rosy reflected as they worked companionably and efficiently through the evening, that she had formed this almost instant rapport with Callum. There had been nothing like it in her life before, nor would be again, an inner voice told her, and her expression grew pensive and a little sad.

'What's wrong?' Callum asked her quietly, putting down his notes.

Rosy focused on him, and realised he had stopped dictating.

'Why should anything be wrong?' she hedged.

'Well, it seems highly unlikely that my exhortation to my students to remember that ultimately economics are about people and not figures should have brought that extremely melancholy look to your face,' Callum told her wryly.

She didn't want to tell him that her sadness had been caused by the knowledge that their lives ultimately would lie apart, and that already she was mourning the loss of the intimacy she was sharing with him. She shook her head in negation of his question, bending over her notebook so that the sleek line of her pageboy hairstyle swung forward, concealing her expression from him, and she didn't see the hard frown that momentarily touched his face, turning his eyes to hard steel.

They worked until just gone midnight, by which time Rosy could see the familiar lines of tension and tiredness drawing deep grooves alongside Callum's mouth.

'Supper?' she asked him quietly, as he leaned back in his chair, closing his eyes, making an almost physical effort to relax.

He shook his head, without opening his eyes, and said huskily, 'What I need right now is a good strong drink, preferably a *couple* of good strong drinks, but that's prohibited under the regime the specialist has me on.' He opened his eyes and looked at her, and she was again amazed by their brilliance without his glasses. 'Something to do with the drugs they've got me on not working with alcohol.'

He moved and winced, rotating his shoulder and then massaging it with his fingers. Tension corded the muscles of his throat, and Rosy ached with sympathy for him.

When she listened to him talking, she forgot how physically frail he was, totally absorbed in the power of his intelligence and conviction, but at times like this, when he was exhausted and drained, when his limp became more pronounced and she was aware of the fever burning patches of dark colour along the far too sharp cheekbones, she felt an almost maternal desire to cosset and protect him.

'Well, if a drink's forbidden, how about some herbal tea?' she suggested, remembering she had seen some in one of the kitchen cupboards. 'If you like, you could go up and get ready for bed and I'll bring it up for you.'

If he was already in bed and starting to relax when he drank the tea, it was likely to have a far more beneficial effect.

He started to protest, getting up and then tensing, unable to stop himself from wincing as pain from his thigh contorted his face and made him curl his fingers in an unconcealable spasm of agony.

Tactfully, Rosy turned her back on him and busied herself with her notebook, saying over her shoulder, 'What time will you have to leave in the morning?'

'About nine.' The words were terse, and she had to fight with herself to stop herself from turning round and offering to help him upstairs. 'I think I will go up.'

The words were measured and slightly indistinct, and Rosy felt her own stomach muscles tighten in sympathetic reaction to the pain she knew he was feeling as she forced herself to say calmly, 'I'll just finish tidying up this lot and then I'll bring you that drink.'

She waited for half an hour, not sure how long it took him to prepare for bed, and then made the tea, camomile, which she knew would be relaxing. She made herself a cup as well, thinking that she could drink it while enjoying a hot bath.

Callum's bedroom door was open. He had left a lamp switched on to illuminate the room. He was already in bed, lying on his back, his head turned towards the window.

As she looked at him, Rosy noted absently that his hair was growing thick and long and would soon need cutting. He turned his head as she approached the bed, and she wondered what it was about his eyes that made her feel so odd inside. For all she knew he was short-sighted, yet they seemed to focus on her with a brilliance that made her feel he could see right into her soul.

'I've brought you the tea,' she told him quietly.

He smiled at her and sat up, the sheet falling away from his body. His skin was faintly olive, his ribs so clearly delineated beneath the flesh that Rosy sucked in a betraying breath of compassion and looked quickly away, not wanting Callum to see her reaction; but it was too late, he was already reaching for the sheet, pulling it back over himself, his voice flat and metallic as he said quietly, 'Sorry about that. I've been manhandled by so many medics that I tend to forget that my body isn't exactly a pretty sight.'

Rosy put down the tea and turned to go, and then remembered how she had felt when Gareth first rejected her... how she had cringed from him, bewildered and hurt, ashamed of her body... and although the circumstances were in no way comparable, she turned back quickly and, before she could change her mind, sat down on the bed and said shakily, 'Callum, I'm sorry. It isn't what you think.'

He looked at her, a tiny flicker of derision burning the depths of his eyes, spurring her on.

'No?' he said tautly. 'I know when a woman's looking at me with revulsion, Rosy—and I don't blame you.'

'It wasn't revulsion,' she checked him angrily. 'It was...' Her mouth had gone dry, and she was quivering inside with a tension she didn't understand as she fumbled for the words to explain the unfamiliar mixture of pain and yearning that had filled her at the sight of his thinness and the knowledge that came with it of how much thinner, how much frailer he must have looked during those awful days when he lay in that makeshift African hospital.

'What?' he jeered, his mouth twisted in an unfamiliar bitterness. 'Pity... disgust...'

She shook her head and whispered huskily, 'No, nothing like that.' She was perilously close to tears, aware of an emotional reaching out within her towards him that was like a flood of painful sensation in her body.

She struggled to find the words and could only say unsteadily, 'It hurt me... inside, to see you and realise...' She gulped and sniffed back the tears filling her throat, and then gave in to the tidal wave of emotion she couldn't control as Callum muttered something above her head and then circled her with his arms, pulling her against him so that her head rested on his shoulder, his hand cupping the back of her head while she sobbed an incoherent explanation against his skin. And she wept even more inwardly as she felt the rapid, feverish race of his heartbeat and wondered why she should feel so strongly about him, yearning to be able to give him some of her own physical strength, fiercely resentful of the betraying wasting of his body and equally fiercely proud of the great strength of his spirit and mind.

The sensation of his hand against her head, burrowing beneath her hair, warmth spreading out from his fingers to her scalp, was pleasurably comforting. One of her own hands was resting on his shoulder, the shoulder that had been so tense earlier, she realised, absently soothing the muscles with her fingers, instinctively seeking to offer him the same caring comfort he was giving her.

Oddly, his muscles seemed to tense rather than relax, and she was just frowning over this peculiarity when she felt his chest move and realised he was saying something to her.

She lifted her head to listen and realised that she had soaked his skin with her cloudburst of tears. Absently she rubbed the dampness away, and saw his face contort. She froze instantly, wondering if she had hurt him, if he had sustained other injuries she knew nothing about. The grooves either side of his mouth had deepened, the flesh white with tension.

'Oh, heavens,' she said shakily, 'I came up here to bring you a relaxing drink, and all I've done is make things worse. I'm sorry about the cloudburst. I don't know what came over me.'

'Too much emotional output, perhaps,' offered Callum.

His voice sounded thicker than usual, husky and faintly rasping, as though his throat was sore.

'I couldn't bear you to think that——' she broke off, her throat tightening with fresh emotion, and then on an impulse which later she couldn't understand at all she bent her head and, with her palms pressed flat against his chest as though she was trying to protect him from any further pain, she touched her mouth tenderly to his stiff shoulder, her eyes misting with tears.

There was no other way she could convey to him what she felt ... how much she ached for all that he had suffered. When she moved back from him and raised her eyes to his face, there were feverish patches of colour burning under his skin, and his eyes when he looked at her glittered with light and pain. He was shivering, too, she realised painfully, hurriedly dragging up the bedclothes and tucking them round him, concern etched in her face as she agonised over the sudden onset of what appeared to be another bout of fever.

'Callum?' she whispered, not sure what she should do.

'It's all right, Rosy,' he told her, his voice cracked and raw, his eyes closed, the sharp grooves alongside his mouth intensified by strain. 'I just need some sleep. I'll be all right in the morning ...'

Taking the hint, Rosy switched off the lamp and then watched him broodingly for half a dozen seconds before walking quietly out of his room.

As she prepared for bed, she wondered what it was that had caused this unexpected and fierce bonding she felt for him; this deep-seated protective urge, this aching awareness of his pain as though it were her own.

It was something for which she couldn't find any logical explanation at all.

CHAPTER SEVEN

Rosy had not expected to sleep well, but she decided when the sound of her alarm pulled her out of a deeply luxurious sleep that her body must be getting accustomed to sleeping in unfamiliar beds. It had been her conscience she had anticipated would keep her awake, but that too seemed to have been more self-indulgent than self-admonitory.

She had set her alarm for seven, intending to be downstairs well before Callum, but, after showering in the pretty bathroom next door to her bedroom and dressing quickly in a flat-pleated soft blue skirt and a short-sleeved cotton knit jumper, she went downstairs to discover that Callum was already in the kitchen.

The sight of him dressed in unfamiliarly formal clothes brought her up short for a moment. The jacket of the grey suit hung from his body like the rest of his clothes, but the fabric was expensive and, unless his tailor was completely blind, must originally have been made to fit him.

She frowned a little, mentally measuring the breadth of his shoulders against Elliott's, since he was the only other man she knew of Callum's height and age, and discovered with a small thrill of shock that, if the suit had originally fitted him, Callum must possess a similar breadth of shoulder and chest to her formidable second cousin.

This discovery had an unexpected effect on the muscles of her stomach, making them feel oddly quivery and weak. She blushed hotly for no reason at all, standing uncertainly in the doorway, her face, although she didn't know it, betraying what she was feeling and her instinct for flight.

'Coffee's made,' Callum told her laconically, and instantly the quivers died, and with them the mental vision she had just had of Callum as he might have been before his illness.

'It was my turn to cook,' she reproached him as she poured herself a mug of the fragrant dark brown liquid and then weakened it with hot milk.

'I haven't forgotten. You can make dinner to-night . . . which reminds me, we must be getting low on food. I normally make one giant expedition a month to get the essentials, and then do the rest once or twice a week as necessary.'

'Well, how about if I take my turn at the monthly shop next time it's due?' Rosy offered generously.

'Done,' Callum agreed promptly, and then grinned at her. 'I was going to do it tomorrow.'

Rosy picked up the tea-towel and hurled it at him, and he ducked, laughing. He looked so different when he laughed, his eyes crinkling up so nicely and his mouth curling so that her own itched to smile in response. He had good white teeth, although one of the front ones had a tiny chip missing, endearingly, so she thought, watching him.

'All right,' she told him, adding threateningly, 'but next time you won't find me as easy to fool.'

No mention had been made of last night, and her spirits suddenly soared, buoyed up by his evi-

dent good humour. She had half expected to find
him morose and withdrawn this morning, knowing
that in his shoes she would probably be dreading
the visit to the specialist and the inevitable poking
and prodding it would surely entail.

'Toast?' she offered, popping some slices of
bread into the toaster. He flicked back the cuff of
his jacket to study his watch, an entirely automatic
and somehow very masculine gesture that focused
her attention on him.

His wrist, while thin, was sinewy and hard-
boned, the contrast of his fine, dark hair against
the crispness of his shirt causing her stomach to
lurch uncomfortably again. The sensation made her
shiver and then frown. She was not totally unfamiliar with sexual awareness, but that she should
experience it for Callum of all people was so ridiculous that it made her smile and wryly question
her body's intelligence.

'Don't think I've got time,' Callum told her. She
saw that the humour had gone from his eyes and
that he was looking very white about the mouth,
as he did when he was in pain or tired, and she felt
a surge of sympathy for him, putting aside the two
pieces of toast and walking over to him.

'Are you sure you don't want me to come with
you?' she offered impetuously, and then bit her lip
as she saw his grim expression.

'I'm not fussing,' she told him defensively, 'I just
thought . . .'

'Well, don't,' he told her curtly, getting up and
heading for the door with long, lithe strides that
made her stare at him in confusion, remembering

his normal awkwardness; but after less than four steps he suddenly halted, all the colour leaving his skin, the bones in his face standing out sharply and painfully, and Rosy realised that he had actually forgotten about his injury and tried to walk normally.

Her instinct was to rush over to him to soothe and help him, but his earlier curtness checked it and she stood immobile, stiff and uncomfortable, sensing his helpless rage and knowing that for some reason she was the cause of it.

He got as far as the door, his limp heavily pronounced, and Rosy's throat ached with tension as she watched him. He stopped and stared at the closed door for what seemed to be a long stretch of time before finally turning to face her.

'I'm sorry,' he said simply. 'I'm afraid I'm a bit on edge. Initially there was a chance that I might lose my leg. There were complications... an attempt to fish out the bullet that went wrong. Luckily for me, once they got me home they were able to put things right. In all of us there are inevitable primitive responses that no amount of civilisation can obliterate. Whenever I have to go and see the specialist it makes me on edge...'

But he hadn't been on edge when she first came into the kitchen, unless his light-heartedness had simply been a means of concealing what he really felt.

She forced a smile that felt as though it was cracking her face in two, and said woodenly, 'It was my fault... I should have realised. I didn't mean to imply that you couldn't manage alone. I just wanted...' She stopped abruptly and looked at him with bleak, devastated eyes as she realised that what she had wanted was simply to be with him. Her mouth trembled and the room blurred in front of her.

She gave a small gasp of impatience at her own weakness and heard Callum make a sound somewhere between a soft groan and a curse, and then realised that he was limping back across the room to her.

'Don't, Rosy,' he told her roughly. And when she smiled and blinked back the tears, shaking her head in negation of her own silliness, he placed his hands on her shoulders and said softly, 'Come on... let's kiss and make up.'

Without even thinking about it, Rosy lifted her face to his as obediently as a child, looking gravely at him while he searched her eyes and then lifted his hands to cup her face.

The warmth from his skin felt comforting, the slight roughness of his fingers against her face creating a frisson of sensation that made her eyes widen and her mouth tremble.

He kissed her lightly, a mere brushing of his mouth against her own; then he lifted his head and looked at her with an expression she couldn't understand.

For the space of a heartbeat something seemed to tremble vulnerably inside her. He moved, his head dipping as though he was going to kiss her again, and she felt the warmth of his breath against her mouth—and then abruptly he released her, stepping back from her.

'I must go. I should be back around four. Are you sure you won't mind being here on your own?'

Rosy shook her head. 'It isn't any more remote than the Dower House,' she told him truthfully, wondering why her voice should sound so rusty and unsteady.

What she had said was quite true, but once he had gone she experienced a loneliness she had never felt before...a restlessness which drew her from room to room as though in search of something, until she realised that what she was looking for was Callum.

That made her go back to the study and concentrate on the work he had left her, but it was done by two o'clock, which left her two hours at least in which to sit and wait for him.

Instead she went out into the garden, vigorously removing weeds until her back ached and her throat felt dry, then she sat back on her heels and studied the lushness of the flowerbeds safely nurtured by the protection of the tall yew hedges behind them. Inside their dark green walls, the plants were protected from the harshness of the wind, proof that, with patience and care and most of all love, almost anything could be accomplished.

She got up and walked blindly to the end of the garden, mounting the solid stile that provided both a seat and a viewpoint from which to study the landscape beyond the garden.

Confusing, unfamiliar feelings were beginning to turn her well-ordered life upside-down. This yearning she felt, this restlessness, just because Callum wasn't here; this fiercely protective awareness she had of his intelligence and his kindness and how very much more worthwhile they were than a macho body and a handsome face; what did all these feelings mean? It would be silly to let herself get too attached to Callum. Their friendship was only going to be temporary; no more than the length of the summer. She should enjoy it for what it was, instead of worrying about how much she was going to miss him when he no longer needed her help with his work.

She shivered a little in the April breeze, grimly aware of her own deep capacity for emotional commitment. If she felt like this about someone who was only a friend, what would she feel if she ever fell deeply in love? She shivered again, acknowledging that it might be better if she never found out, half envying Callum his ability to cast aside his sexuality and live his life without the tormenting burden of desire.

Questioningly she wondered if he had ever been in love, and, if so, if it was experiencing that love that had turned him into the celibate recluse William had unwittingly described to her. If so, the woman who had rejected him must have been a fool to so carelessly throw away all that Callum had to offer. Of course, it was true that he was not good-looking, especially not now, with his bony, too thin frame and his uneven shock of dark hair which, now that it was growing, drew attention to the high arch of his cheekbones and the hardness of his jaw.

It was five o'clock—time for her to start making dinner. She went inside and inspected the fridge and freezer. No wonder Callum had said they needed supplies; the fridge was empty of anything other than a couple of packets of butter and a few tomatoes, while the freezer was equally depleted.

There were plenty of eggs, though, and some bacon, and a rather hard piece of cheese, and she decided that she could probably make an omelette.

She wondered if Callum would have had lunch in London, or whether, like her, his nerves would have prevented him from eating, and finally, as she assembled her ingredients and then stared unseeingly out of the window, she acknowledged that she had been on edge all day, not just because she missed him, but because she was concerned for him . . . worried about him.

She wasn't concerned when he wasn't home by half-past five—after all, he had only said around four—but it got to six and then seven, and the flutters in her stomach had become an insistent churning that wouldn't let her rest.

When the phone rang, it sent a thrill of fear right through her. She picked up the receiver with fingers that shook visibly, giving the number in a clipped, anxious voice.

'Rosy. . . Rosy?'

Her body sagged with relief. It was Callum, and he sounded as though he was smiling. She pictured him in her head, his eyes crinkling at the corners, his mouth curling. She could hear odd sounds in the distance, and realised that it was the hum of conversation and the clattering of china and cutlery.

'Rosy, are you OK?'

That should have been her line, she thought wryly, nodding and then realising that he couldn't see her, and saying hastily, 'Yes, I'm fine.'

'I've got a bit involved... Some old friends have persuaded me to join them for dinner. I may stay overnight... I don't know. Will you be OK?'

She stared at the receiver, stunned by how hurt she felt, frowning over her own emotions, and then, before she could reply, she heard a low, sultry female voice saying huskily, 'Darling, do come on... I'm dying for a drink.'

Darling... She swallowed hard, her body trembling with anger. All this time she had been sitting here worrying about him, while he...

'Rosy?'

'I'll be fine,' she told him curtly. 'Have a nice evening.'

She wasn't going to ask him how he had got on with the specialist. Let the owner of that sultry, sexy voice do that, she thought viciously, slamming the receiver down. Let *her* watch with her heart in her mouth and a pain in her chest while he walked with that awkwardness that betrayed his pain... Let *her*... She stopped herself abruptly. What on earth was wrong with her? She was behaving as though Callum was in some way her private property. Of course he had every right to dine with friends and stay overnight in London if he chose. Her face burned as she realised how churlishly she had behaved. She could only pray that he hadn't recognised the curtness in her voice for what it was. He had sounded so light-hearted and happy.

Bleakly she wandered into the kitchen, surveying the preparations she had made for dinner.

Suddenly she no longer felt hungry. She cleared the table and made herself a cup of coffee, nursing it broodingly. The evening stretched out barrenly ahead of her, making her realise how much she had come to look forward to the long, informative discussions she shared with Callum.

At nine o'clock she decided that a walk might help ease her tension. It was dark outside, and the lane beyond the house led nowhere, petering out after a couple of miles. In the other direction it led to the main road and then to the village four miles away.

It was the evening when the bell-ringers had their practice, the sound reaching out across the countryside, melodious and slightly haunting.

Rosy had no fear of the empty countryside. She had grown up in such surroundings, in the hills of Northumberland.

She walked for half an hour, breathing in the clean air, trying to rationalise her muddled thoughts. She wasn't sure she understood what was happening to her, and she feared that she was perhaps in danger of transferring to Callum all the emotionalism she had felt on discovering Elliott's existence; but Callum was *not* a member of her family and, even if he had been, it was both immature and unfair of her to try to burden another human being with her own loneliness.

She wondered if she might perhaps be suffering from some sort of emotional fallout from Great-Aunt Maud's death, if her awareness that she was now virtually alone in the world had in some way caused this inner yearning... If so, she must find a way of combating it.

It was still only ten o'clock, too early really to go to bed. She went into the sitting-room and switched on the television, but none of the programmes could hold her attention, and at eleven she acknowledged that there was no easy cure for her restlessness and went to bed, willing herself to fall asleep.

When she did, some time after twelve, it was so deeply that she had no awareness of the powerful engine of the Mercedes whispering quietly up the lane. Not even the clunk of its door closing penetrated her dreams, and when Callum walked quietly into her room her face was turned towards the moonlight shining through the curtains, her breathing as even and deep as a child's.

He watched her for several moments, standing between her and the light, and when she moved in her sleep, dislodging the bedclothes, he tugged them back, gently covering her creamy-skinned shoulder, smiling a little grimly at the demureness of her broderie anglaise nightdress with its tiny ribbon straps.

By rights he ought to be in London. A chance meeting with a reporter he had met in Ethiopia had led to an invitation to dinner and the chance to renew acquaintances with Lucy Grendon, a photographer he had also met in Ethiopia.

Lucy was thirty years old, divorced, and determined not to repeat the mistake of her marriage. She had red hair and a temper to match, and she had been coldly disapproving when Tim Pearson's wife, Anna, had tried to pair them off together.

Much as he liked both Tim and Lucy, Anna wasn't his type, a sultry, vivacious brunette who liked to play the vamp, especially when her husband was watching. Callum winced, flexing his forearm, remembering how hard her long fingernails had dug into him as she'd dragged him away from the telephone.

Tim had offered him a bed for the night . . . there had been no real need for him to cut the evening short and come racing back. And then he smiled to himself, a grim, savage smile that would have stunned Rosy had she seen it, as he questioned his own understanding of the word 'need' and reached out tentatively to touch the curve of Rosy's cheek. So intelligent and quick, and at the same time so naïve and innocent . . . It was a lethal combination—where he was concerned, at any rate. He moved back from the bed, wincing as he put too much pressure on his injured leg. According to his specialist it was healing well, but there was a long, livid scar and an unsightly puckering of flesh that looked and felt unpleasant.

He remembered Rosy's comments about his celibacy, and grimaced to himself. A man suffering from the injuries and pain he had experienced was hardly likely to experience physical desire, and before that . . . before Ethiopia . . . too many female undergraduates, with more on their mind than coaching in economics, had made him cautious and careful to keep his private life completely separate from his work. He thought about Rosy's years at university, and wondered if the Welshman had ever realised what he had thrown away.

He also wondered a little thoughtfully about Elliott Chalmers. Rosy had said that she didn't love him sexually and he believed her. She was still unawakened ... unaware ...

She murmured in her sleep, and said something that made him stiffen as he recognised his own name. She was frowning, and as she turned over the covers slipped again, this time almost to her waist.

When his heart had stopped thudding audibly in his own ears, he acknowledged that the broderie anglaise was not as prim as he had first imagined. It was in fact a new nightdress, purchased especially for Rosy's visit to Bea and Elliott, and it had a pretty matching robe. At home she had worn comfortable old nightshirts, or, in the summer, nothing at all. Her nightdress had come from a small shop in York specialising in pretty underwear. It had a low-cut front and a bodice that laced together over a demurely gathered skirt. The set had been reduced and Rosy had been persuaded into buying it, not realising until she put it on, long after she had bought it, how far from demure it actually was. It had been designed for a bride's trousseau, and the bodice was cut very low and shaped in such a way that it coaxed her breasts to swell over the ribbon edging. The bow that tied the front lacing invited the eye, suggesting temptingly that with very little effort indeed it could be easily untied, revealing the soft fullness of her breasts.

Callum found it difficult to breathe and realised that he was actually holding his breath. He released it unsteadily, freezing as Rosy moved again, screwing her nose up as though she was going to sneeze. The movement of her body dragged the cotton bodice downwards, revealing the dark aureoles of her nipples.

Callum reached out towards the bedclothes and then stopped, unable to trust himself to cover her up without touching her. He shouldn't even be in her room at all, he told himself grimly, moving silently away from the bed.

Rosy woke with her alarm, but made no effort to get up. What was the point? Callum wasn't here. She yawned and sighed. Her dreams had been confused and unhappy, leaving her feeling melancholy.

She sat up in bed and then tensed as she heard a brief rap on her door.

It opened and Callum walked in. She stared at him in shock, making no attempt, as she would normally have done, to either reach for her robe or slide down beneath the protection of the bedclothes.

'You're back,' was all she could say, while pleasure clamoured inside her, and her melancholia lifted.

'I came back last night,' Callum told her. 'You'd already gone to bed. I was up early, so I thought I'd bring you a cup of tea.'

Now, as he limped over to the bed, she became aware of her semi-nudity, and her skin flushed delicately, but Callum seemed so unaware and uninterested in her that she fought back the impulse to huddle under the bedclothes and asked huskily instead, 'Your leg... What did the specialist say?'

'That it's getting better,' he told her promptly. 'He's suggested a week of intensive physiotherapy on a residential course, to strengthen the muscles, and then some exercises I'll be able to do myself to add to the benefit of the course.'

'A residential course. Does that mean you'll be going away?' Rosy asked bleakly, the pleasure draining out of her as she contemplated a week without him.

'It looks like it. He hasn't given me a final date yet,' Callum said casually. He put her tea down on the bedside-table next to her and sat down on her bed. Automatically she moved her legs to make room for him, too upset now as she thought of him going away to think of anything else, least of all the brevity of the bodice of her nightdress.

'He's given me a ninety-nine-per-cent chance of fully recovering the use of the leg muscles,' he told her calmly, 'but only if I work to combat the wasting effect of the injury. Of course, there'll always be some scarring... I could have plastic surgery, but the thought of another operation...'

'Plastic surgery...what on earth for?' Rosy asked him, appalled that he should even think of putting himself through further physical pain.

'The scar isn't exactly a pretty sight,' he told her quietly.

'But surely that doesn't worry you?' Rosy began to protest, but he interrupted her, saying curtly,

'No, it doesn't bother *me*, but it isn't exactly the sort of thing I'd want to reveal to someone else.'

He saw the confusion in her eyes and explained bluntly, 'It neither looks nor feels pleasant, Rosy. In a situation where a woman might want to touch me...it isn't exactly conducive to adding to her desire. Rather the opposite.'

Rosy stared at him, and then a slow, hot crawl of colour seeped up under her skin, turning her scarlet.

'You mean if you were making love,' she managed to say shakily, mortified by her embarrassment, but knowing it was impossible for her to hide it. 'But I thought...you said...'

'You thought I was celibate,' Callum supplied briskly for her. 'And that's true now, but it may not always be.'

Her throat burned, and so did her eyes. She felt sick and her stomach twisted unbearably with sharp pain.

Her reaction to the thought of Callum with a lover appalled her. All she could manage was a numb, 'If she...loves you...it won't matter about the scar,' and she was not really surprised by the grim look he gave her. She sounded like a naïve schoolgirl full of romantic ideals which had no bearing at all on real life. 'I'd better get up,' she said wildly.

'Er—not yet...' Callum leaned across her, preventing her from throwing off the bedclothes.

She stared at him. He wasn't wearing his glasses and she could see the light dots of hazel in the darker green of his iris.

As she looked at him, his eyes seemed to glow and mesmerise her. Her gaze dropped to his mouth.

He was smiling slightly. She wondered what it would be like to touch that curling mouth with her fingertips.

From a distance she heard him saying drily, 'I think it might be a good idea if you stay exactly where you are until I've gone. For my sake rather than yours.' And then, to her shock, she felt his fingertip tracing a line just above the neckline of her nightdress on the warm, naked curve of her breasts. His finger dipped to the hollow between her breasts, stroking lightly against the skin where the laced ribbons tied, unimpeded by the fabric that should have stopped him. Rosy looked down and saw that the bow had come unfastened and that any movement, any movement at all was going to drag the two panels of the bodice apart and fully reveal her breasts.

She took a deep, shaky breath, looked wildly at Callum while her face burned.

'I'd offer to fasten it for you, but I'm not sure I've got the will-power to resist the temptation it offers,' he told her simply, standing up.

After he was gone, Rosy wondered wildly how long it had been unfastened. The ribbons were silky satin, and it wasn't the first time the bow had come apart. As she showered and dressed, she balled the nightdress up and vowed that she would throw it away.

Oh, lord, how could she face Callum after something so embarrassing? But if he hadn't stopped her, if she had moved... Her skin flushed.

Reflected in the mirror was the full lushness of her breasts revealed as Callum would have seen them if he hadn't. She tensed and trembled, re-living the sensation of his finger stroking gently across her skin, and then her face burned as she saw her body's physical response to the memory in the sharp peaking of her nipples.

And then she wondered unhappily why Callum had touched her, and if it had anything to do with the sultry-voiced woman she had heard over the telephone, and the fact that he had come home instead of staying overnight in London.

Had she, that woman, rejected him, and had he, Callum, come back feeling...? But no, she wasn't going to let her mind wander down those forbidden avenues, she told herself firmly.

CHAPTER EIGHT

FOR most of the morning, Callum shut himself away in the sitting-room, reading through the notes Rosy had typed the previous day. He had given Rosy some references he wanted her to check, which kept her busy searching through the various textbooks he had mentioned.

He had a phenomenal memory, she reflected, when she had nearly completed the list, and in every case the text he had used exactly matched the reference he had asked her to check.

She imagined that he would be a good lecturer, making the subject come alive for his students.

She didn't see him again until lunchtime, when they ate the omelette she had intended to prepare the previous evening. Afterwards she left for Oxford armed with a long shopping list and what seemed to be an extremely large sum of money.

Of course, she was only used to shopping for herself and Great-Aunt Maud, and the kitchen garden at the Dower House had kept them well-supplied with all the vegetables and salad ingredients they needed. A local farmer had supplied them with eggs and since, during the last months of her illness, her great-aunt had only been able to tolerate the most bland of diets, their food bill had not been particularly large.

After she had parked her car in the large car park attached to the supermarket, she glanced at her list. Callum had offered her the Mercedes, pointing out that there was more room in the boot for her shopping, but Rosy had explained to him that she felt more at home driving her own car.

She noticed as she checked the list that it showed a healthy awareness of what went to make up a well-balanced diet. She had seen already that Callum shared her own preference for fish as opposed to red meat.

As she inspected the fresh vegetable produce, she mourned the Dower House's kitchen garden and grimaced a little distastefully over some tomatoes, admitting that having been used to them fresh from the greenhouse, rich in scent and flavour, her taste-buds had been rather spoiled.

Thinking about her home reminded her that she must ring her solicitor to ask him if he could arrange for the police to continue their weekly check on the house until the end of the summer.

It wasn't worth while letting it for that short period, and even though she had gone through Great-Aunt Maud's things after her death there were still small personal items of her aunt's in the house that the latter wouldn't have wanted anyone else to touch. Her embroidery frame, for one thing . . . the china teacup in which she always liked her afternoon tea . . . the spectacle case which had been a present from her parents, and other small, personal treasures, which Rosy hadn't been able to bear putting away.

Another symptom of her loneliness, she admitted, as she joined the queue behind the till. While her aunt's things were still scattered round the house, it made her feel as though she wasn't completely alone.

She wondered idly what Callum would think of the Dower House. It was rather larger than his cottage, a small Queen Anne building in soft red brick with stone-framed windows neatly aligned one above the other, with a third storey of dormer windows in the roof. Inside, on the first two floors, the rooms were neat and rectangular with high ceilings. The front door opened into a square hall and a pretty, lacy staircase floated up to a galleried landing. Rosy loved the house, but it was a feminine, pretty place, lacking the robust colour and warmth of Bea and Elliott's home and the warm, comforting untidiness of Callum's.

Puffing a little after loading her cardboard boxes into the boot of her car, Rosy straightened up, stretching her spine and her brain as she tried to think of a less stressful way of transferring supermarket shopping from trolley to car and then, at the other end, from car boot to shelves.

As she got into her car and started the engine, she watched a young mother, who had just stored her food in her own car, deftly transferring a toddler and a baby into safety seats, and decided wryly that equality between the sexes would actually have arrived the day when it was the male of the species who was in the majority at supermarket car parks, dealing with the mundane day-to-day activities that made life flow smoothly.

The shopping had taken her longer than she had expected, and it was late afternoon when she finally turned off the road and into the lane to the cottage. She frowned as she saw an unfamiliar car parked outside: a bright yellow Citroën, like a brilliantly shelled snail.

As she unsnapped her seat-belt, she decided that if Callum had visitors she would go straight to the study without interrupting them, but as soon as she had walked into the kitchen she heard Callum call out from the sitting-room, 'Rosy, is that you?'

She could scarcely ignore him, so she walked towards the sitting-room door and then stood there and stared as she saw William and Chrissie sitting on the settee. Chrissie looked quite at home, but William looked tense and uncomfortable, and Rosy wondered what on earth was going on.

'Are you there, darling?'

She hadn't realised Callum had got up until he came across to her and slid his arm round her, moving her surprisingly deftly so that his body shielded her from the others.

As his head bent towards her, he murmured in her ear, 'It's all right...I think William just wanted to check that you were OK.'

Callum was only reassuring her, and of course the other two would expect him to greet her as a lover, but an unexpected trickle of panic began inside her as his mouth left her ear and moved lazily along her jaw.

His hand was resting against her heart and he must be able to feel its frantic thud. He moved it and she started to breathe more easily, waiting for him to step away from her, but instead his hand cupped her face, while the arm holding her against him tightened and he whispered against her mouth, 'There's nothing to be afraid of, Rosy. I'm not going to hurt you.'

The words sent tiny quivers of sensation racing through her body. It was almost as though he was kissing her already... her eyes closed involuntarily, her lips softening. He caressed them slowly, learning their shape and vulnerability, the hand cupping her face suddenly tensing so that she opened her eyes and stared at him. Her heart was thudding erratically, her body as weak and light as air; a confused, muzzy sensation seemed to be dulling her brain and, instead of saying something... instead of moving away and acknowledging William and Chrissie's presence, all she could do was stand there, her tongue moistening her lips, while she trembled with confusion and uncertainty.

When Callum leaned his forehead on hers and gently reached out and touched her mouth with his fingers, a long shudder wrenched through her. She was breathing hard as though she had been running, she recognised numbly, transferring her stunned gaze from Callum's face to where her fingers were curled into the fabric of his shirt. How had that happened? She had no memory at all of reaching out to touch him, never mind clinging to him with fingers which she could only uncurl with a tremendous effort of will, and even then her hand remained flat against the fabric of his shirt, feeling the fierce beat of his heart.

It was only Chrissie's cheerful, 'My goodness . . . I think you and I had better go, William,' that brought her back to reality. She jerked away from Callum, wondering if she looked as visibly stunned as she felt.

William was saying something, but she couldn't concentrate on the words. Callum responded to him, speaking evenly and mildly, and Rosy realised they were discussing Bea and Elliott's visit.

'Bea's worried because she hasn't heard from you,' she heard William saying stiffly to her, and she bit her bottom lip guiltily. She had intended to ring Bea, but somehow or other had kept putting off doing so.

'That's my fault,' she heard Callum saying easily, as he came to stand behind her, putting both hands on her shoulders. She wanted to lean back against him. Her bones felt as weak as water, and the warmth from his body lapped round her comfortingly. 'I thought we'd wait until their visit so that we could surprise them with our news.'

What news? Rosy wondered dazedly, but she hadn't got the strength to ask. Callum was gently drawing her back against him as though he had read her desire. His hands moved from her shoulders to her midriff before sliding to her waist. He moved, shifting his weight slightly. She felt the taut stretching of the muscles in his thighs where she lay against them as she trembled at the unfamiliar intimacy.

'William says your cousin and his wife are arriving on Friday. I'll book a table for us,' he announced, mentioning a particularly good restaurant in Oxford.

He was still holding her against him, smoothing her hip idly with one hand while he spoke, and Rosy, catching sight of their reflection in the french window, had to acknowledge that they looked exactly like the lovers they were supposed to be.

'Satisfied now, mother hen?' Chrissie asked William forthrightly. Rosy couldn't look at him. She felt uncomfortable about deceiving him, which was ridiculous really when the whole thing was partly his fault.

'We've got to go,' Chrissie told Rosy. 'There's a debate tonight I want to hear and the car's only on loan. Oh, before we leave, may I use the bathroom?'

The cottage had no downstairs cloakroom, and she started to pull away from Callum.

'It's upstairs... I'll show you.'

Callum let her go, and she was half-way upstairs with Chrissie at her heels before she remembered that the bathroom was next door to her bedroom, and that her things were scattered all over it, and that she had left the bedroom door open. She faltered, wondering wildly how on earth she could explain away the fact that she and Callum had separate rooms.

She walked past Callum's door. His room had its own bathroom, a luxury thoughtfully installed by the previous owners, who had made use of the small boxroom, converting it into a master-suite bathroom.

Behind her Chrissie was chattering gaily, telling her what a pain William had been since she left, saying he was beginning to turn into an old woman. 'Honestly, I told him the days of wicked men stealing innocent girls away to sell them to white slavers are over...' She giggled and added thoughtfully, 'It's more likely to be the other way round.'

They had reached her bedroom and Rosy stopped abruptly. The door was open as she had left it, the bed neatly made, but her robe and slippers and sweater she had left on the back of the chair, the book she had left on the bedside-table, were gone. The room looked as though it had never been used.

'Bathroom's here,' she told Chrissie unsteadily. 'Er... would you like me to wait, or can you find your own way back?'

Chrissie paused, her hand on the bathroom door. Inside, the bathroom, like the bedroom, was free of the intimate feminine clutter Rosy had left there. She blinked and stared, not really listening while Chrissie said teasingly, 'It's OK... there's no need to wait. You go and rescue Callum from William. Honestly, he's worse than a Victorian father.'

Rosy's legs were oddly unsteady as she made her way back downstairs. William was standing up, his spine ramrod-stiff, his expression still wary.

He greeted her with a searching look that reminded her a little of Elliott, even though there was no blood connection between the two. When he matured, William was going to be a rather formidable male, she recognised, a little surprised.

'Everything all right?' Callum asked her softly, reaching for her hand and uncurling her fingers with his own. He smiled at her and his eyes crinkled. She tried to smile back, but her face felt too stiff.

Chrissie came downstairs noisily, her manner ebullient as she teased William.

'Honestly, he hasn't let me have a moment's peace until I agreed to drive him out here,' she complained, as Callum and Rosy accompanied them out to her car.

The whole thing rattled when she started the engine, and in the passenger seat William sat hunched up and severe. Rosy wanted to reach out and tell him not to worry. She felt guilty because she hadn't rung Bea, but she had been terrified that her lies would stick in her throat and that Bea would immediately realise something was going on.

Now she acknowledged that she was going to have to ring her. She tried to focus her mind and imagine what she would say and do if she were in love with Callum.

But if she were in love with him, she doubted that she would simply have moved in with him after such a short acquaintance. It was not in her nature. She was too cautious . . . too much a product of her upbringing. She would have needed a steady period of courtship before she could be convinced that he loved her. And then there would have been the trauma of explaining to him her lack of experience...her fear that he would cease to love her when he discovered that she was still a virgin. They would have had to have made love before she moved in with him, because she would never have allowed herself to risk being rejected should he find her ignorance a turn-off as Gareth had done.

And more than that . . . her nature was not one that would allow her to cast herself rapturously and adventurously on the high seas of life. If she had fallen in love with Callum, she would have wanted to feel that their relationship would endure, that it would be something they would build into the future with marriage and children, not something ephemeral which she was content to experience for the mere stretch of one summer.

She started to shiver as Chrissie drove away down the lane. Callum was still holding her hand.

'I'm sorry about that,' she apologised tensely, pulling her hand away and turning back to the house, so that she didn't have at look at him. 'I had no idea William would do anything like that. What on earth did he want?'

'What he wanted was to find out exactly what my intentions towards you are.'

Rosy stopped in her tracks, so that Callum, who was following her into the kitchen, almost bumped into her.

'What? Oh, Callum, no! What on earth did you say to him?'

'Let's go and sit down,' he suggested quietly, and Rosy thought she heard tiredness in his voice and chided herself for allowing him to stand for so long, worrying that he might have overstretched damaged muscles.

Numbly she allowed him to guide her into the sitting-room, staring at him as he pushed her gently into a chair and then went over to the old-fashioned oak chest that was set into the wall and opened one of the doors to remove a bottle of sherry and a couple of glasses.

'Here—drink this.' He passed her a glass of the pale gold liquid, and Rosy, who rarely touched alcohol, Great-Aunt Maud having disapproved of women drinking, took a gulp and then swallowed, gasping slightly as the sherry warmed her throat and stomach.

'Sherry,' Callum told her severely, 'should be sipped, not gulped.'

He sat down opposite her, holding the glass in both hands, studying its contents for several seconds before saying quietly, 'I should have anticipated something like this, but I'm afraid I hadn't. William took me rather by surprise, and I'm afraid I said the only thing I could think of on the spur of the moment.' He paused, and Rosy felt her stomach lurch. 'I told him that we were getting engaged . . . that we intended to announce our plans over dinner with your family. . .'

Rosy's hand shook, spilling some of the sherry on to her skirt, but she didn't notice.

'I'm sorry,' Callum apologised abruptly, getting up and walking over to the window, his back to her. 'It seemed the best thing to do. In his shoes, I doubt that I would be very pleased to discover that a member of my family might be taken advantage of in her innocence. At his age, I'm not sure I would have had the guts to do what he did. I rather suspect not.' He gave her his illuminating heart-wrenching smile.

'My background wasn't so very dissimilar to yours. My parents were in their forties when I arrived. My father was a Presbyterian minister in a rather remote part of the Scottish Highlands. He and my mother were gentle, almost innocent souls, and until I left home to go to university I had a very limited experience of life.

'My parents are both dead now; they died within months of one another, my father from a heart attack and my mother, I suspect, from grief. I don't have any close family, just some distant cousins in New Zealand...'

It was the most he had ever told her about his personal life. Half of her wanted to question him, to find out if his childhood had been a happy one... to see if, like her, he had been largely unaware of any aloneness until it was really too late to change the habits of upbringing; to discover if his experiences in any way paralleled hers; but the other half was too urgently and hotly angry with William to allow the questions to be asked.

As though he knew what she was thinking, Callum said gently, 'Don't be angry with William. His heart's in the right place.'

'Is it?' Rosy challenged. 'First he thinks I'm trying to break up his sister's marriage, and now...now this. What would have happened if you and I were really in love, Callum? How do you think I'd feel, coming home to discover that someone who isn't even really related to me had been here questioning your intentions towards me? How do you think I'd feel...knowing that you were being pressured into a commitment that you might not be ready to make? What if William's inter-

ference had made you back off from me because
you weren't ready for that kind of commitment?'

He had turned round to look at her, and Rosy
could see that he was angry. He came over to her
and took hold of her shoulders.

'Listen to me, Rosy,' he told her grimly. 'If you
ever do fall in love with someone, and he isn't prepared to commit himself to you one hundred and
fifty per cent, then he isn't worthy of you.

'Tell me something honestly. If you were in love,
wouldn't you want commitment, permanency...
marriage and all that goes with it?'

Rosy moistened her lips. How well he read her.
What he was saying only mirrored what she herself
had just been thinking.

'Yes,' she agreed dully. 'But men these days...'

'Would you have come here to live with me as
my lover without knowing that I shared that
commitment?' he continued ruthlessly, ignoring her
attempt to speak.

She shook her head, knowing that there was little
point in lying to him.

'No,' he agreed savagely. 'And neither would I
have asked you. I'm well past the age when what
I want from a relationship is sexual experimentation. William was quite right to ask what he
did,' he finished quietly. 'And I think it's just as
well that he did.'

Rosy's head jerked up.

'Don't you see?' Callum asked her quietly. 'If
William can see so clearly that neither of us is the
type to indulge in a brief sexual liaison, then how
much more evident must that have been to your

cousin? A man of subtle and keen intellect, from all that you've told me about him; William certainly seems to hold him in awe. Would he have believed that you had moved in here with me out of mere sexual desire?' He shook his head.

'That's all very well,' Rosy burst out frantically. 'But you've told William that we're getting engaged, and now Bea and Elliott will expect us to make plans.'

'And you're terrified that you might find yourself trapped in a marriage you don't want? Don't worry. We'll tell your family that we aren't making any plans to marry until after I'm fully fit. I think your cousin will understand that male pride won't allow me to marry you before that happens. After a suitable length of time, you can tell your family that I'm going to be left with a permanent disability and that in the circumstances...'

Rosy was staring at him in horrified fury. Her voice trembled with it as she demanded breathlessly, 'You expect me to tell them that I'm walking out on you because you might have a limp?'

'It isn't unheard of, Rosy,' he told her gently. 'Your sex can be just as demanding of physical perfection as mine, you know. Look, let's not worry about how we're going to end the engagement now. Let's just concentrate on how we're going to convince your family that it actually exists. I'd better get you a ring.' He was frowning thoughtfully. 'I'll do that tomorrow. I have to go in to Oxford anyway. I've got a meeting with the Dean to discuss my syllabus for the coming term.

'Oh, by the way, in case you were wondering... I've dumped all your stuff in my room. It seemed wisest.'

'You knew that Chrissie would want to go upstairs?' Rosy asked him.

He shrugged. 'I didn't know, but it seemed a fair possibility, which brings me to another point. I think it might be a good idea if you sleep in my room until after your cousin's visit is over.' He saw her face and said grimly, 'It's all right, Rosy. I won't be sharing it with you. We'll work out a rota for the bathroom, and I'll leave my stuff in there so that if we get any more surprise visits we'll be prepared for them. I'll sleep in one of the other rooms.'

Rosy gazed at him. It seemed incredible that he should be prepared to go to such lengths, and all for her benefit. She said as much, faltering over the words until his eyebrows rose and he said humorously, 'Rosy, I am only human and I've no objection at all to people thinking that a very beautiful woman loves me. It's a pity I can't persuade you to stay and marry me. It would be an ideal way to keep the more ardent of my female students at bay.'

Ignoring his teasing, Rosy frowned. It gave her an unpleasant pang to think of him surrounded by nubile, eager young women all too ready to flirt with their tutor. She had seen it happen when she was at university herself. The attraction had nothing to do with the man's looks, but rather the charisma and power he represented. It was a pattern that many otherwise intelligent women went on repeating throughout their lives, more often than not with unhappy consequences.

'I can't let you do this,' she protested huskily. 'I'll tell Bea and Elliott the truth...'

But her face went white as she thought of having to do so, and when Callum said firmly, 'It's too late, Rosy. There's no going back,' she allowed herself to be convinced that somehow or other they would find a way out of the situation when the time came to do so.

'I'd better go and unpack the car. What would you like for dinner?'

'I thought we'd go out,' Callum told her, adding wickedly, 'to celebrate our engagement; but first I'd better go and do these exercises I'm supposed to do.'

It took her over half an hour to empty the car and stack everything away, and then she made some fresh coffee; wondering if Callum wanted some, she went upstairs to ask him.

His bedroom door was open and he was lying on the bed with his back to her, wearing only a pair of briefs, his hand resting on his thigh as though it hurt.

She could see that he had been exercising. His hair was damp with sweat, his skin flushed. He was completely still and she wondered suddenly if he was all right, or if he had overdone things and passed out.

Impulsively she hurried across to the bed, kneeling on it, so that she could reach over to him, saying urgently, 'Callum, are you all right?'

His eyes had been closed, but as she spoke they opened quickly, his pupils dark and shocked. He wasn't wearing his glasses and he reached for them, swinging his legs off the bed. As he moved, Rosy saw the scar on his thigh. She sucked in her breath as she saw the puckered, damaged flesh.

'Repulsive, isn't it?' Callum asked her harshly, suddenly still. 'Just the kind of thing to give a sensitive soul like you nightmares.'

He was angry, but beneath his anger she could sense anguish and she said softly, 'No, it isn't repulsive at all.'

'Oh, come on! I saw your face. You practically went green.'

'Because I couldn't help thinking how it must have hurt you,' she told him honestly, and, without realising what she intended to do, she reached out and touched him tenderly, tracing the scarring with her fingertips, until he moved violently and snatched her hand away, holding her wrist in a grip that bruised.

'All right, so you can bring yourself to touch me...just about. Nurses and doctors have touched me, Rosy...because to them I'm just another lump of human flesh...a set of injuries that have to be mended. All of us have our dreams, and I've got to face up to the fact that from now on I can only make love in the dark. No woman is going to be able to make love to me without feeling revulsion the moment she sees that scar.'

'You're wrong,' Rosy told him unsteadily.

His mouth compressed, curling sardonically. 'You think so?' he mocked her bitterly. 'You think a woman is going to want to touch me there with her hands...with her mouth...'

Rosy felt as though her stomach had fallen into a bottomless pit. Her face burned and her heart pounded as she was forced to confront the erotic images his words drew. She knew he was trying to embarrass her into backing down and admitting that he was right, but she wasn't going to let him do it.

Staunchly she stood her ground, refusing to give in to the bitter challenge in his eyes, and before she could lose her courage she leaned over him and slowly placed her hand over the puckered, seamed flesh, watching Callum steadily while she did so. When he cursed and moved violently, gripping her hand and dragging it away, she flinched from the look in his eyes but didn't let it sway her determination, bending her head until the silky swing of her hair brushed his skin and then flowed over it, touching with her mouth first the outer edges of the scar and then slowly moving inwards, ignoring the rolling sensation of panic attacking her stomach and the biting grip of Callum's fingers as they dug into her shoulder.

He tried to drag her away, but she resisted, knowing that, since he couldn't move her without hurting her, he wouldn't do so, and then, when her lips trembled against the heart of the puckered scar, she felt him shudder violently and she realised how much she had violated his privacy and exactly what she was doing. Her hand rested on his thigh, the muscle compacted into grim rejection beneath her touch, and as the realisation of what she was doing flooded through her she became aware of other sensations: the hard warmth of his skin, the unfamiliarity of flesh covered in fine, dark hairs that prickled her hand, the rapid pulse beneath his skin, the scent of him, warm and male, known and yet unknown.

The stillness between them seemed to stretch into eternity, and yet later she knew it must have lasted only seconds, and then Callum groaned and beneath her hand his tormented muscles twitched. His fingers circled her arms, drawing her up the bed.

'Rosy, what the hell do you think you're doing?' he cursed. But he didn't let her reply. Instead he kissed her, not gently as he had done before, but violently almost, grinding his mouth down over hers until her lips swelled and parted, and he caught the bottom one between his teeth, biting into its softness in a way that made her pulses leap and her body arch like a bow, instinct taking over from reason so that, in her already highly emotional state, she had no defence against the floodtide of sensation that picked her up and carried her in its turbulence.

Beneath Callum's mouth her own opened, her hands finding the damp heat of his chest and smoothing it with frantic, undirected movements that drew a sound from his throat which made her shiver convulsively and welcome the intimate invasion of his tongue.

He pushed her flat on the bed and held her there while he kissed her, his body arching over her own, both protector and hunter. His skin burned against her palms. She tried to open her eyes to look at him, but her eyelids felt as though they were sealed with leaded weights. His tongue touched her swollen mouth. His teeth tugged slowly on her bottom lip.

She shivered, mindlessly swamped by sensation as his mouth caressed her jaw and then her throat; her body moved urgently. His hand spanned her throat, his thumb measuring the frantic pulse of her blood. Her hands sought purchase on the sweat-slick slope of his chest and slid helplessly to his waist.

His mouth touched the pulse in her throat and she quivered with wild pleasure.

'Rosy...' She felt the reverberation of her own name through her body, and, like a child not wanting to be woken from a happy dream, as she felt him draw away she captured his hand and placed it against her breast, keeping her eyes squeezed tightly closed, feeling the hammer-beats of her heart and the shallowness of her breathing, waiting with a tension like nothing she had known before. Willing him not to withdraw from her.

CHAPTER NINE

'ROSY,' he said again, and his voice was sombre with warning.

She had forgotten that when she first saw him she had pitied him ... considered him sexually unattractive. All she knew was the desire that burned inside her: a white-hot, searing need that had come from nowhere, but which intuition told her belonged to him. Just the weight of his breath against her skin made her body crawl with sensation ... with an agonising, unbearable need for him. His hand rested lightly against her breast where she had placed it, cupped slightly so that he was barely touching her. Beneath her shuttered eyelids she had a mental vision of her body as she had seen it that morning after he had touched her: her breasts bare and swollen, her nipples distended and hard. She shook violently, letting her imagination tell her what she might feel had he touched her then, and, opening her eyes, she arched up against him so that even through her blouse and bra she could feel the pressure of his hand.

'Touch me, Callum,' she begged him. 'Touch me.'

She saw his eyes darken and knew that she had reached him ... touched the male core of him and awakened desire in him. She burned under the slow inspection of his scrutiny, feeling the hot sear of it as though it physically burned.

From a distance she heard him saying thickly, 'How do you want me to touch you, Rosy? Like this?'

And, almost miraculously, his hands had laid bare the full swell of her breasts and the narrowness of her ribcage, her blouse unbuttoned and already sliding from her shoulders so that it was no effort at all to remove it, as his hands cupped her breasts and slowly explored their soft contours.

She was sitting up and Callum was kneeling in front of her.

'Like this?'

The sensation of his thumb tracing the outline of her nipple through the fine silk of her bra made her cry out and arch her back, pushing herself into his hands, frantic for him to tear away the barrier of fabric and satisfy the ache that spread from her breasts to the centre of her body, pulsing unremittingly there so that she was no longer Rosy, but merely a tormented, aching thing of need beyond any kind of rational constructive thinking.

She heard Callum say something and, fearing that he was going to abandon her, she reached up with a strength she hadn't known she had possessed, digging her fingers into the muscles of his shoulders, pulling him down until his mouth rested against the upper slope of her breasts.

She felt the tension run through him like coiling wire, and swiftly the need clouding her mind and obscuring reality faded. She shuddered, appalled by what she was doing, unclenching her fingers from his body, staring at the downbent darkness of his head with appalled, dazed eyes. She was shivering with reaction, and a chill of self-disgust that shook her crawled through her stomach like sickness.

Callum raised his head and touched her face gently. She wanted to look away from him, but she couldn't.

'It's all right, Rosy. It's all right,' he told her, but it wasn't, and nothing could be all right ever again. She had no idea what had happened to her. Like a totally unknown force, desire had swept over her. From making a gesture of generosity and affection, from wanting to show Callum that his body was not repulsive, she had gone swiftly to a need so intense that her mind couldn't cope with it. And now the need had gone, like a violent sickness of such horrendous proportions that she could hardly believe it had been there. But it had been, and she had... She moaned softly with despair and tried to pull away from him, but he wouldn't let her go.

'Rosy...' His voice soothed and calmed her, penetrating the wall of self-loathing inside her.

'I...I don't understand what happened,' she told him helplessly. 'I never meant...'

'I know.'

She had the feeling that he did. She searched his face and saw nothing there other than the familiar warmth and kindness, and the pounding of her heart started to ease, the sickness dying away.

'I've never done anything like that before. Never felt that... Never wanted...' She shuddered, and her glance fell on his thigh. She wanted to touch it again, as though by doing so she might understand where her passion had come from.

'I just came to see if you wanted a cup of coffee,' she added in a bewildered voice.

'How disappointing, when I thought you'd intended to seduce me.' She tensed in shock, and then recognised the familiar, teasing note beneath the laconic words. 'Rosy, you don't have to explain,' he told her quietly. 'I understand.'

He was so calm, so natural, for all the world as though they were downstairs in his study instead of sitting on his bed, her blouse a discarded scrap of fabric on the floor and he wearing only his briefs.

'I wish *I* did,' she told him shakily, taking courage from his placid lack of reaction.

Something flickered in his eyes and her own faltered. She wondered what it was she had said to make them flare hotly like that.

She moistened her lips, bemused to find them still swollen from his kiss.

'I—I'd better go.'

'In a minute,' he agreed. 'Let's have a little talk first.'

Panic flared inside her. He's going to send me away, she thought instantly, and then wondered why that should be her first thought and fear.

He picked up one of the pillows and pushed it against the bedhead, so that he could lean on it, and then patted the space next to him and said, 'Come and sit here. We might as well be comfortable.'

Gingerly Rosy moved towards him, careful to preserve a distance between their bodies and flushing when he cast her an amused glance and teased softly, 'I'm not combustible, you know. You won't burst into flames, simply sitting next to me.'

When the hot colour flooded her skin and she stayed where she was, her face sick with tension, he groaned and said ruefully, 'Rosy, stop looking at me as though you think I'm about to beat you. I know you're very...innocent, but you surely know better than to think that I would be anything but flattered by what happened.'

Her fingers curled in an agony of embarrassment. She didn't want to talk about it. She felt terrible. How could she have done such a thing? How could she have...? She closed her eyes and opened them again as Callum reached out and slid an arm round her, firmly tucking her against his side, and exhibiting a physical strength that surely was something at odds with his thin frame?

Only it wasn't quite as thin as it had been, Rosy recognised, unable to resist the firm pressure of his arm and finding that it was much easier to let her head rest against his shoulder than to keep on struggling to sit up straight.

'Right, now we're sitting comfortably, I'll begin,' Callum intoned, and even without looking at him she could hear the smile in his voice. 'There's a rapport between you and me, Rosy, that both of us would be fools to deny. Maybe it's because both of us know what it's like to be alone in the world; maybe it's because both of us for one reason or another have experienced an alienation from our peers.

'Probably we'll never know. What I do know is that you were the first woman since the accident to look at me without embarrassment or pity.'

'Was there someone . . . special in your life before you were injured?' Rosy asked him hesitantly.

She felt his tension, and had a sinking awareness of having guessed correctly.

'What makes you ask?'

'I just thought that that might be the reason for your . . . your celibacy. If you had loved someone and they had . . . been unable to . . . Well, you said that most women would be turned off by your injuries.'

'Was that why you touched me, Rosy?' he asked her softly. 'Was it because you thought I might be hurting inside because of someone else?'

'Partly,' she agreed. 'But then everything changed and it wasn't because of you any more. It was because of me . . . what I felt . . . what I needed.' She stopped and asked him shakily, 'Callum, why did I feel like that? I've never . . .'

As though he knew how upset she felt, he touched her mouth with his fingers, sealing the impulsive words away, and said, 'Think, Rosy. You've been under a tremendous amount of emotional pressure. Your aunt's death . . . the discovery that you had a second cousin, Elliott. Your happiness at being welcomed into his family, and then the pain of finding that your feelings towards him had been totally misunderstood. A lot of things have happened to you in a short space of time. And today hasn't helped. All those emotions have been building away inside and had to be released.'

He was so calm and matter-of-fact about it, so kind and thoughtful.

'I am sorry,' she told him. 'You must have been appalled.'

'Oh, yes, I was,' he agreed. 'A very beautiful young woman asks me to...'

He broke off as he felt her shudder, tilting her face so that he could see the tears clustering on her lashes.

'Oh, Rosy, you fool. Do you really know what I thought...what I thought and felt? I thought it would be heaven to remove this obtrusive piece of fabric from between us,' he whispered against her ear, his fingertips lightly touching the strap of her bra, 'so that I could see if you looked as wonderful as you felt. I thought it would probably send me crazy if I touched you with my mouth, but I was going to anyway. I was going to kiss you here, just where this teasing swell of flesh had been tormenting me.' His finger traced lightly along the edge of her bra, raising a shivery rash of sensation. 'And then, if by some miracle you hadn't stopped me, I was going to taste you here,' his thumb unerringly found her nipple, circling it lightly, the gentle pressure making her catch her breath in shock as her flesh hardened and pushed against her bra, 'to see if you were as sensitively responsive as you seemed. And, what's more, I'd thought all that before you'd said a word,' he told her. 'You see, you weren't alone, Rosy.'

'But when I first touched you, you pushed me away,' she managed to say when her heart had stopped racing in shock.

'Because you were arousing me,' he told her quietly, watching the colour come and go in her face. 'As a matter of fact,' he continued conversationally, 'you're arousing me now.'

She couldn't help it; her glance shifted betrayingly from his face to his body, drawing a soft laugh from him that made her blush.

'Well, Rosy,' he teased her, 'shall we go out to dinner, or shall we stay here and make love?'

She knew it was meant to be a joke, but suddenly she realised what it could mean to her if he did make love to her. She would be free. With Callum, there wouldn't be any need for explanations or worries. She needn't fear rejection, or not being able to please.

They weren't in love, so there was no pressure on her emotionally to arouse his desire and sustain it through the discovery of her ignorance.

With Callum, she could learn everything that she didn't know. She looked at him and said huskily, before she could change her mind, 'I'd like to stay here and make love.'

She knew she had surprised him. She saw it in the widening of his eyes and their involuntary darkening. Before he could speak, she rushed on nervously. 'Callum, don't you see, with you it won't be like it would be with someone else?'

'Because you'd love this someone else?' he asked flatly, and she had the strong impression that he was furious with her, even though he was concealing it from her.

'You were just pretending when you said I aroused you, weren't you?' she challenged. 'You were just saying it to make me feel better.'

'No, damn you, I wasn't,' he denied roughly. 'Rosy, I can't let you do this.' He took her face in his hands and looked into her eyes, his expression serious. 'You haven't thought it through.'

'You *were* lying,' Rosy said chokily. 'You say you're my friend. If you were, you'd understand that I don't want to spend my life alone. That I want to give and receive love...that I want a husband and children. Stop pretending, Callum. You don't desire me, and neither will any other man.'

She started to turn away from him, but he stopped her, gripping her arms and looking at her with such a mixture of anger and pain that she trembled. 'For pity's sake, Rosy, I'm only human,' he told her roughly. 'And I do want you. I want your body against mine, without any barriers between us,' he told her softly, unclipping her bra and peeling it away...

'*Any* barriers,' he repeated softly, tugging the zip of her skirt, making love to her with his voice, while his hands stripped her body of her clothes and then furnished it with another kind of covering that was fire and ice, light and dark, invisible and yet felt in every tiny nerve-ending of her skin as his hands stroked over her and the same surging pulse of desire she had felt before came flooding back, as easily summoned by his touch as though he had command of every force within the universe; and within the universe that was her body, he did, she recognised dazedly.

'What shall I teach you first, Rosy?' he murmured into her ear. 'How I can make you feel when I do this?'

She shuddered as his hand spanned her breast, his thumb against her nipple, the friction of its movement against her flesh causing spasms of sensation to leap from her breast to her womb as he lay with her, watching what he was doing to her.

'Or would you like to know how you can make me feel if you touch me in the same way? I'd like to feel your hands against my body... and your mouth.' He saw her shudder and his eyes darkened.

'Everything you do... even that... arouses me.' His teeth touched her ear and she trembled violently. He put her hands on his chest and kept them there while his mouth caressed her throat, making her arch and dig her nails into his skin without knowing she was doing so. His tongue stroked her breast and then her nipple. She moaned deep in her throat. His mouth opened over her tormented flesh, tasting it slowly and then gently releasing her. She lay there staring at him, panting for breath, quivering from head to foot.

'Now you do the same to me.'

She did as he told her, uncertainly at first until she felt the contraction of his muscles as her mouth touched his flesh, her tongue exploring the hardness of his flat nipple. And then she discovered that the sensation of his flesh within her mouth and his reaction to her caress was so intensely exciting that she didn't want to stop, so she kept on kissing him, pressing eager, open-mouthed caresses against his skin, until he stopped her, pushing her down on the bed with a roughness that startled her, covering the hardened tip of her breast with his mouth and sucking on it until she screamed softly with pleasure, whimpering deep in her throat as he refused to let her go, but kept on savaging her with desire until her whole body pulsed with the ache inside her and her nails scored wildly against his flesh.

His hand on her waist, her belly and then between her legs was something she welcomed instinctively, letting him touch her as he wished, knowing only that what he did, she wanted, and that every time he touched her he only seemed to anticipate what she would have asked him to do had she known the words.

She wanted to touch him as he was touching her, to make him feel the pleasure he was giving her. She pressed her palms against the slick dampness of his skin, exploring it hungrily, wild with a need to communicate to him how he was making her feel.

He raised his head and turned, watching where her hand lay against his skin.

'Help me, Callum,' she whispered uncertainly. 'Show me what to do to make you feel what I feel...'

'I don't need to show you,' he told her, and his voice shook. 'You already know.'

She looked at him blankly, not understanding, and he told her rawly, 'Everything you do arouses me, Rosy. Everything.' And then he kissed her, sliding his palms along her jaw, teasing her mouth with his tongue and then imprisoning her with the weight of his body as he kissed her properly.

Every inch of her welcomed the silken pressure of his weight, every inch of her sang joyously at the intimate contact of flesh on flesh.

When he released her mouth, her heart was thudding, her heartbeats quick and fast. She bent her head and kissed his shoulder.

She wanted to taste every part of his flesh, to absorb its different textures through her fingertips and mouth, to know all there was to know, so that when he was no longer there she could close her eyes and remember.

'Rosy...' He said her name softly, a mere breath of sound, and then kissed her breasts gently, once and then once again, and her heart kicked fiercely.

'We can't do this,' he told her softly. 'Neither of us has any protection. I could make you pregnant... Unless...'

She almost lied to him and told him that she was on the pill. Instead she said truthfully, 'I ... I think it would be safe enough.'

Something hot and fierce flared in his eyes.

'You're willing to take that risk?' he asked softly. 'The risk of conceiving my child?'

Conceiving his child. Her stomach melted and she went boneless. Odd how much the words affected her. Almost as odd as that earlier desire she had had to treasure every memory of him she could make. Surely only a woman in love would feel like this? Only a woman in love would...? The breath squeezed out of her lungs, leaving them hurting and tight. Callum was waiting for her to say something, gently stroking the hair away from her face, watching her. Quickly she veiled her eyes, dropping her lashes to cover her thoughts.

'There isn't much risk,' she told him huskily, absently almost, her thoughts elsewhere.

'Have you any idea how much you're tempting me?' he whispered into her throat. And just the sensation of his breath against her skin made her body quicken until she felt a tiny tremor convulse her womb. Her lips parted, her breathing ragged and shallow. His hands slid over her skin and he whispered things to her that made her frantic with wanting him. She kissed his throat, tasting the salt of his sweat, feeling the muscles ridge, knowing that when she slid her hands over his chest the fierce hammering of his heart was caused by her touch.

He was gentle with her and patient, encouraging her tentative caresses, letting her grow in self-confidence, so that the sudden clamping of his fingers round her wrists when she touched the hard flatness of his belly shocked her.

Her body trembled, fearing rejection...fearing that he had been lying to her, after all.

'I want you, Rosy,' he told her, releasing one wrist and tracing the trembling curve of her mouth with his fingertip, as though unable to stop himself. 'When you touch me like that I can't think straight. If you want this to stop, you've got to say so now.'

She trembled between caution and need, and need won. He saw it in her eyes and expelled his breath on a ragged sound that made her stomach muscles lock.

He moved and she realised he was removing his briefs. She wanted to look at him, and yet felt shy.

'Touch me now,' he murmured against her mouth, 'and let me show you exactly what it does to me to have your hands on my skin.'

When she didn't, he laughed softly, taking her hands and placing them low on his stomach, as though he knew she wanted to touch him, despite her hesitation.

He kissed her slowly, teasing her lips, tasting her mouth, easing his tongue between her lips and moving inside her mouth with lazy, erotic insistence that she suddenly realised was mimicking the movement of his hips against her body, dragging his flesh against her hand until her fingertips touched the crispness of his body hair and then the hard rigid heat of him, pulsing beneath her hand.

'Rosy, Rosy, Rosy...' He muttered her name in a paean of praise, punctuated by kisses, his heart slamming, his fingers touching her as intimately as she was touching him.

She tensed and gasped beneath their sensual stroking, wondering if he could feel the urgency that was gripping her, wondering at the softening, quivering sensation inside her body.

And then she couldn't think any more as he touched the small, hard nub of flesh he had unerringly found, coaxing it, stroking it until she started to shudder and tremble, not releasing her even though she pleaded with him to do so. She was terrified by the way her body was going out of control, fighting against the spasms of sensation building up inside her, until he covered her mouth with his, destroying her resistance with the fierce pressure of his kiss and the rocking movement of his body as he forced her to give in to the surges of sensation inside her.

It wasn't what she had expected. She had wanted to feel him inside her, and despite the pleasure she felt cheated...cheated too of knowing she had given him the same satisfaction he had given her. But when she tried to tell him, to protest raggedly at what he had done, he held her tightly and said against her mouth, 'Shush, Rosy, it isn't over...I just wanted to give you pleasure first. It isn't always so good the first time. I didn't want you to be disappointed.'

And then he moved and her eyes widened as she felt the powerful surge of his body against hers. Automatically her hips lifted to receive him, her legs and arms wrapped round him as he groaned and moved into her, filling her, stretching her, making her want to accommodate all there was of him.

She had forgotten that there might be pain, and felt it only in a single sharp pang that she noted with surprise and then forgot as her body quickly adapted itself to new pleasures, and she discovered that by sliding her hands down Callum's back she could make him twist and arch and move inside her so that she felt delicious tremors of pleasure.

Tremors that built up quickly and explosively once he realised that he wasn't hurting her and began to move powerfully and forcefully inside her, showing her how to respond to him, how to move with him, so that the sudden, shattering convulsions of sensation came almost before she knew what was happening, and her body clung eagerly to his, robbing him of any hope of self-control as he cried out her name, a harsh, almost tortured sound of release.

She slept, protected by his arms, the reassuring beat of his heart against her skin, unaware of how long he remained awake, watching her, brooding on what he had done, cursing himself for giving in to temptation.

When she woke up she was alone. It was dark outside. She looked at her watch. Midnight ... Callum must have gone to bed in another room. She wished he had stayed with her. She wanted him with her, she recognised, and then wondered why she had not realised until now that she loved him.

Her heart jolted against her breastbone, and against her closed eyelids she could see vivid images of him as he made love to her.

Everything she had been taught by her great-aunt said that what had happened between them was wrong, but an older, wiser knowledge said no, it had been right: a gift given by him to her, if not in love, then at least with love—the love of one good friend for another.

CHAPTER TEN

'ROSY.' She sat upright in bed, as Callum called her name and then came into the room.

'I've brought you a cup of tea. Rosy, about last night . . .'

She couldn't look at him, and her hand trembled a little bit as she took the mug.

'I don't regret what happened, Callum,' she told him quietly. And then, because she didn't want to burden him any more than she had done already, she crossed her fingers under the bedclothes childishly and lied, 'You've given me the freedom to be able to fall in love without the fear of rejection. One day, when I'm an old, married woman with half a dozen children, I'll look back on yesterday and be even more grateful to you than I am now,' she joked.

'Grateful . . .' he interrupted her grimly, coming towards her and placing one hand on the bedhead as he leaned over her.

The scent of him, which she must have been breathing in all the time she worked with him without feeling the way she did this morning, made her tense nervously, terrified that the feelings inside her would overcome her self-control, and that she might reach out and touch him. She couldn't bear to look at him, frightened of what she might betray if she did.

He had given her so much; she had no right to give him the additional burden of her love. He was so scrupulously compassionate and responsible that if he guessed how she felt he would feel obliged to send her away. His work wasn't finished and she suspected that, without her, he would drive himself far too hard.

She felt his free hand touch her shoulder, cupping it firmly, his fingers warm against her skin, and she jumped as though he had stabbed her with a red-hot needle, pulling away from him, turning her head just in time to see his face settle into a mask of hard withdrawal.

'I'm sorry,' he said distantly, standing away from the bed.

For what? she wanted to ask him. For making love to me...for showing me just what the physical relationship between man and woman can be...for showing me what love can be? She wanted to tell him that *she* was the one who was sorry, but she was frightened her voice would betray her, and so she shook her head instead.

'I take it that yesterday is something you now want to forget,' Callum said tersely.

Forget? Never. But for *his* sake...

She tried to force a smile and to match his cool approach.

'Yes, I think that would be best. Not because I regret what happened...I don't...'

There was a long silence when she could feel him willing her to look directly at him, but she couldn't. At last he said quietly and violently, 'Well, at least there's no pretence any more that we're lovers, which should make things a damn sight easier when we meet your cousin.'

Lovers... Something shivered inside her, a sweet, slow pain that made her both want to laugh and cry at the same time.

She had wanted things to be the same, but they weren't, and she acknowledged that one of life's most painful lessons was that there was no going back...no wiping out of life's errors. *She* might not have regrets, but Callum had; she could feel them in the tension that hummed between them; in the loss of that special easy intimacy they had previously shared...see it in the brooding way he watched when he thought she didn't know; and in her heart the pain grew and flourished until it shadowed every aspect of her life with him.

There were no more eager debates after dinner...no more shared evenings spent in front of the sitting-room fire; Callum shut himself away in his study instead.

And then it was Friday and they were going out to dinner with Elliott and Bea.

Bea rang her just after lunch to say that they had arrived, and in her voice Rosy could sense all the questions she wanted to ask. But her conversation was light and tactful. William had told them about her job... It had been a surprise to receive her letter telling them that she and Callum were in love. They were both looking forward to meeting him.

In turn, Rosy asked after Henrietta and the children, both those born and those as yet unborn, but there was a distance between her and Bea now, a knowledge in her own heart of things that could not be discussed.

After she had put down the receiver, Bea turned to Elliott and said worriedly, 'Something's wrong. She isn't happy. Oh, Elliott, we should never have let her come to Oxford with William.'

Elliott frowned grimly. He had just had a long and extremely illuminating interview with William, and was mentally cursing himself.

'Don't worry,' he told Bea, squeezing her hand gently. 'If need be, we'll rescue her and take her home with us. Let's wait and see what this evening brings first, though, shall we?'

Upstairs in her room...*Callum's* room, Rosy studied her reflection in the mirror and frowned over the pallor of her skin. Her dress, a simple silk wrap affair with long sleeves and an almost businesslike bodice in her favourite shade of blue, with a skirt that draped cleverly to enhance the slenderness of her hips and legs, seemed loose on her. She nibbled worriedly at her bottom lip, wondering if others would see the strain in her eyes as clearly as she could herself.

She found her shoes, high-heeled sandals that matched the dress, touched her pulse-points with her favourite perfume and checked her make-up. It was half-past seven, the time they were due to leave. There was nothing to stop her going downstairs, but she didn't want to.

In four short days so much had changed. Then she had known that Callum would somehow convince Elliott that they were in love; she had hated the deception, but felt no dread of it being exposed. Now it was different. Now she feared that neither of them would be able to play their roles convincingly. Callum, who before had shown her affection and warmth with the occasional brief touch of his hand... with his closeness to her, whether it was simply when they were standing together checking his notes, or after dinner, when he would pat the space on the settee next to him, wanting her to sit next to him rather than on a separate chair, now maintained a distance between them that hurt her every time she noticed it. No longer did he push her hair behind her ear when it swung over her face. No longer did he perch on her chair while she was working, leaning over her so that their bodies touched when he pointed something out to her. No longer did he envelop her in warmth and laughter, and she felt the chill of its absence like the lack of a warm protective cloak in a cold east wind.

How on earth was Elliott going to be convinced that they were lovers, when Callum couldn't endure to so much as touch her with his fingertips?

She was still standing in the bedroom when she heard the rap on the door. She looked at it uncomprehendingly. Since that morning when he had brought her the tea and they had agreed that those brief hours of pleasure he had given her were to be forgotten, he hadn't come into the bedroom at all.

She opened the door uncertainly, her eyes registering the shock of seeing him dressed formally in a dinner-suit. It seemed to fit him better than the rest of his clothes, or had he perhaps put on a little bit of weight? He was standing upright, which made him look taller, taller and broader, the brilliant white front of his shirt dazzling her eyes.

If she had seen him like this the first time she met him, she would never have approached him, she recognised. She would have been too overawed, too intimidated. He wasn't wearing his glasses, and his hair when he turned his head was overlong and shaggy, brushing unevenly against his shirt-collar.

'You'll need this,' he told her brusquely, presenting her with a small, square jeweller's box. She looked at it and then at him, trembling inside.

He had said she would need an engagement ring the day William had visited them, and then no further mention had been made of it. She had anticipated that he would buy a cheap trinket of fake stones, but she knew when she opened the box that this ring was no fake.

There was no gaudy flash of brilliant stones, just the subtle appeal of old gold, surrounding an amethyst as deep and dark as a lakeland tarn, reflecting the purple hue of the surrounding heather.

Intricate lovers' knots in strands of gold surrounded the stone, a delicate balance to its richness.

It was beautiful; just what she would have chosen herself. Her hand trembled and she almost dropped the box. She closed her eyes, willing the tears crowding her eyes not to fall. She heard Callum curse, and then the box was taken from her with the same suppressed violence she could see in so many of his actions now.

'Here. You'll have to wear it,' he told her curtly. 'They'll be expecting it. I don't suppose William will have kept quiet about our plans.'

And before she could stop him he had taken her left hand and put the ring on it.

Despair almost choked her. She looked blindly at her hand, her face white.

'You shouldn't have done that . . .'

He seemed to understand immediately what she had meant, because he said savagely, 'Why not, Rosy? Because that privilege was one you were reserving for the man who eventually makes you his wife? What an odd creature you are. Quite happy to give me your body, and yet you go sick with revulsion because I touch your hand.'

He sounded so ferally dangerous that she couldn't speak. She had never imagined he could feel such anger, or express it. It was like looking at another man. A man who wore a tortured mask that lent his face only a grim resemblance to Callum's familiar features. What had happened to his gentleness . . . his compassion . . . his understanding?

'Come on,' he told her grimly. 'Let's get this damned farce over with.'

They were driving to Oxford in Callum's car, not hers. He drove well, concentrating on the traffic, leaving her to dwell painfully on the bitterness he had shown her. She shouldn't be letting this happen. She turned to him to tell him so, but he forestalled her, saying harshly, 'It's too late to change your mind, Rosy. We're committed now.'

Committed . . . She suppressed a small, hysterical laugh. *She* was committed, all right . . . committed to him body and soul for the rest of her life; but it was a commitment he did not want.

The whole evening was going to be a nightmare.

Bea and Elliott had arrived at the restaurant ahead of them. Rosy made the introductions, watching as Elliott and Callum studied one another. Two very strong men measuring one another's weaknesses and strengths.

Callum's manner towards Bea was everything she had expected: gentle, kind, appreciative of her womanhood and her very special gifts.

When the rest of them ordered drinks, Callum shook his head, explaining easily that he was not really allowed to drink because of the strong drugs he was still taking.

From there the conversation turned to his time in Ethiopia, Elliott putting shrewd and informed questions to him, so that for a while Bea and Rosy were excluded from the conversation.

'I like him,' Bea whispered to Rosy encouragingly. 'I'm so happy for you, Rosy...' She glanced at Rosy's left hand and her smile deepened. 'You're wearing your ring. William did mention that you were getting engaged, but we weren't sure if it was official yet...'

Rosy didn't realise that both men were listening to them until Elliott said calmly, 'I hope you aren't intending to rush her into marriage, Callum. Having only just found my new second cousin, I'm in no rush to lose her. How long will it be before this work Rosy's doing for you is finished?'

'Not much longer now,' said Rosy truthfully, un-settled by the grim, almost bitter look Callum gave her.

'Good. Bea and I were going to suggest that you come back to live with us, Rosy. It will give you both a breather before the wedding.'

Rosy gaped at him, and looked uncertainly at Callum.

'I think Elliott is trying to warn us that he doesn't entirely approve of us living together,' Callum told her, watching her face as the colour came and went in it.

'It isn't for me to approve or disapprove,' Elliott countered.

'No, it isn't, is it?' Callum agreed pleasantly, and Rosy shifted uncomfortably in her seat, wishing she had never got herself involved in this situation. Nothing was turning out as she had planned.

The restaurant had a small dance-floor. After they had had their meal, Bea and Elliott took advantage of it, Elliott holding his wife so lovingly that Rosy felt the ever-present tears clog her throat.

She dared not look at Callum. He and Elliott had been fencing verbally with one another all evening, and the atmosphere was not a comfortable one. If she and Callum had actually been in love, she dreaded to think how he might have reacted to Elliott's subtle challenges to him to prove the per-manency of his feelings for her.

She was sitting staring at the dance-floor when she heard a woman saying huskily behind her, 'Callum, darling . . . what a wonderful surprise!'

She tensed immediately, recognising the voice. It was the woman she had heard over the telephone when Callum had been in London. She turned her head and looked at her. Tall, soignée...closer to Callum's age then hers, beautifully made-up and expensively dressed, she seemed to float across the distance that separated them, leaving the party she was with to reach out to Callum with both hands, and then kiss him lingeringly on the mouth.

'How much better you're looking. Quite like your old self,' she approved, sitting down, ignoring Rosy. 'Darling, why on earth did you rush off like that the other night? It wasn't because you were jealous of Tim, was it?' She pouted provocatively, long, slim fingers resting on Callum's arm, smoothing the dark fabric with deliberate caresses that turned Rosy's stomach over. She had never contemplated murder before, but she was contemplating it now. This was the woman who was responsible for Callum's pain...this was the woman who had rejected him. This was the woman he loved, she recognised bleakly, watching helplessly as she flirted with him, coaxing and teasing, touching him at every opportunity while she talked about past events...past friends...deliberately excluding Rosy from their intimacy.

'Look, I'm going to be staying in Oxford for a few weeks. Why don't I come and see you?' she purred invitingly.

'Impossible, I'm afraid. I'm going away tomorrow. A course of treatment for my injuries.'

Rosy had almost forgotten about Callum's residential course of physiotherapy, and she blinked at him, feeling as though the bottom had just dropped out of her world. A week without him . . . the rest of her life without him.

The woman was saying something about them keeping in touch. He was holding her at bay now. Through pride probably more than anything else, but he loved her, Rosy knew, and how long would he be able to withstand the pressure of her desire and his love? How long before he asked her to leave because he wanted this other woman in all the ways he would never want her?

How could she stand to simply stay and wait, a helpless victim unable to defend herself from the blow she knew was going to fall?

She heard Callum say something to her, and looked at him numbly, realising that the other woman had gone.

'I was asking if you wanted to dance,' he repeated icily, realising she hadn't heard his original question.

She shook her head, unable to look at him. There was no way she could trust herself to remain calm and in control if he held her in his arms. Just the thought of being so close to him after the misery of the last few days made her legs tremble. Once in his arms, she would betray herself and he would know it, and then there would be no end to her pain and humiliation.

She saw that her refusal hadn't pleased him. His mouth drew into a tight, hard line, and she suspected he would have made some unkind comment if Bea and Elliott hadn't returned.

It was relatively early when they left, Rosy more than glad to escape both Bea's concerned, affectionate glances, and Elliott's shrewder, more dangerous ones.

Neither of them spoke a word on the drive back. When Callum unlocked the back door, she was almost half-way up the stairs before he halted her, saying grimly, 'You know I'm off early in the morning.'

'Yes.' She had her back to him. She dared not turn round and look at him.

'Rosy...'

Was that really pain in his voice, or was it just weariness? She ached to turn round and go to him...to beg him to understand and forgive her, but she just couldn't.

'I'm tired, Callum,' she said tightly, ignoring the softening tone. 'I want to go to bed.'

Just for a moment she thought he might come after her. She felt the tension in the harsh breath he expelled, but once she moved he made no attempt to stop her.

She was awake nearly all night, making plans and then discarding them, but by daylight she knew what she was going to do. Even though she was awake, she waited until Callum had left before getting up.

She packed her things slowly and mechanically, as though what she was doing wasn't actually real.

By lunchtime she was on her way, returning to the place she called home, knowing that, for her, home was no longer a place but a person, and that person was Callum.

She had been home for two days before she was able to write to Bea. Her letter was brief, simply saying that the engagement was off and that she had gone home.

Writing to Callum was harder. She tore up half a dozen stilted conventional explanations that were an insult to herself and to him, and then, in a mood of angry defiance, sat down again and this time wrote the truth.

She told him honestly that she hadn't meant to deceive him, that she hadn't known until it was too late that she loved him and that she wasn't writing to him now to burden him with her feelings, simply to explain that she accepted that he loved someone else and that she felt for both their sakes that it was better this way.

The letter would be waiting for him when he got home, and she tried not to think about him walking into the kitchen, limping a little, perhaps, tired from the long drive, slitting the envelope, and frowning over it as he read its contents.

She tried not to visualise his relief when he realised that she had gone and that there was not going to be any uncomfortable necessity for him to explain to her that he wanted her to leave.

She even tortured herself by wondering how long he would be able to hold out against his sultry-voiced lover. Not very long. She would coax him and tease him, and press that voluptuous red mouth against his, and because he loved her he would forget that she had once rejected him and deserted him and he would welcome her back into his heart and his life.

She was crying by the time she had finished picturing this scene, tears that seemed to well up out of nowhere and pour down her face as though they would never stop.

There was no phone call from Bea...no acknowledgement of her letter. The week went past drearily, and despite the fact that physically she kept herself so busy that she was exhausted, she found that at night she was unable to sleep.

On Saturday she had been home for a week. It was a warm day, warm enough for her to work relentlessly in the garden, driving herself so physically hard that when she stopped mid-afternoon for a drink she fell asleep on the lawn, unaware of the day's lengthening shadows or the soft purr of the expensive car as it crunched down along the Dower House's gravel drive.

Callum had had a long, uncomfortable journey; two journeys, if he counted the drive back from the exclusive and expensive health hydro where he had spent the last week. His leg ached from the punishing exercises he had undergone; his new mobility had been gained only at a price. He had been told that with time and patience the pain would go and the strengthening muscles remain.

He was tired now; tired and angry with the kind of anger that comes from overwhelming relief from fear.

He tried the door, and got no response. Rosy's car was parked outside the house. A wall ran alongside the front of the house, extending the line of it. There was a door in it, half-open, tempting the eye. The sun was slipping down low on the northern hills, casting soft shadows. The air up here was clean and sharp. Beautiful countryside, proud and austere.

He walked into the walled garden, the breath catching painfully in his throat as he saw Rosy lying on the grass.

Asleep, she looked as she must have done as a child. The promise of summer in the strength of the sun had dusted freckles across her nose. He studied her for several minutes, torn between anger and joy, as much against himself as against her.

That murderous drive home, desperately needing to know why she hadn't answered the phone. Finding the letter...then driving over to see her cousin. An uncomfortable interview with Elliott Chalmers, until he put his cards on the table, and told him exactly how he felt, and then the impatient, agonising drive to Northumberland.

He leaned over her and said her name quietly. She didn't waken, but a tear slid down her face. Not a child at all, but a woman. More of a woman than he had ever expected to know.

'Rosy,' he said again, and this time she opened her eyes.

'Callum!' She couldn't believe it...Callum here. She sat up weakly, wincing as pins and needles burned the arm she had been lying on.

Her senses absorbed his presence greedily. He was carrying extra weight ... extra muscle. He had had his hair cut, and her heart turned over like a leaping salmon. He looked so physically male, so very much the antithesis of the man she had first seen beneath the apple tree in his wheelchair. He moved, levering his weight from one leg to the other, and she saw him wince.

Immediately she got up.

'You're not well. Callum...'

His eyes mocked her, taunting her slightly, and she knew, if she had not betrayed it already, that her words, her face... her every gesture must have told him how she felt.

'I'm well enough to feel like throttling you for your idiocy,' he told her wryly. 'Rosy, you fool. What on earth gave you the idea that I was in love with Anna?'

She stared wildly at him, uncertain of what he was trying to say.

'Aren't you? I thought she must be the one... who rejected you after... after the accident.'

He sighed and sat down on the stone bench which was sheltered by the height of the yew hedge behind it, reaching for her and tugging her to her feet, and from them to the seat beside him.

'Rosy, no one rejected me. I simply let you think that because... well, because it made things far less complicated. You assumed I lived the life of a celibate monk. I knew that if I told you that my "celibacy" was simply something I projected as a defence against the amorous advances of some of my students you'd take flight, and since that was the last thing I wanted you to do...'

He sighed and reached for her hand, turning it over and studying the soft palm, tracing her heartline with his forefinger, the light touch making her tremble.

'I must confess, I never realised the problems it would lead to. Anna was simply someone I knew. She and I were never more than mere acquaintances, but she's the kind of woman who, once she decides she wants a particular man, simply refuses to admit that her desire isn't reciprocated.'

He felt the tension in her body, and continued carefully.

'You, on the other hand, are exactly the opposite, and won't accept or believe that you *are* desired. And not just desired...'

He saw her chest rise quickly as she fought to breathe, and said urgently, 'Rosy, for goodness' sake look at me. This is the first time I've ever told a woman I love her, and it's like walking on a tightrope without a safety net.'

She looked at him, as he had known she would, and he took her other hand, holding them both firmly.

'Rosy, I could murder you. How dare you let me think that you didn't care? How dare you flinch away from me every time I came near you...and most of all, how dare you run away while I wasn't there to do anything about it?'

Her mouth trembled and she couldn't speak. She shook her head, lowering it so that he couldn't see her face. She heard him make a rough sound of exasperation and frustration, and then she was in his arms, feeling the fierce thud of his heart and the arousal of his body as he muttered threateningly, 'Don't you dare do anything like this to me again.' And then his self-control shattered and he found her mouth, kissing her with a naked hunger he made no attempt to disguise.

'I've loved you from the first moment I saw you,' he told her between kisses. 'Why on earth do you think I was so determined to keep you with me?'

He lifted his head and saw the bewilderment in her eyes.

'No human being is that philanthropic,' he told her drily, and then added, 'Do you really believe I would have made love to you otherwise?'

'You didn't want to...'

'Like hell,' he told her inelegantly. 'I wanted to that day in Richard's garden. I wanted to pick you up and lay you down in the grass and watch the expressions chase themselves through your eyes as I gave you pleasure upon pleasure, but I knew then you didn't see me as a physically desirable man.' His mouth twitched. 'It's vain of me, I know, but I decided then that one day you'd look at me and want me; and then, when you did, I realised that I loved you and I didn't want to take what you were so innocently offering. I thought it was too soon. I wanted to wait until you loved me, but I couldn't...'

'Was that why you were so angry the next day?' Rosy asked him, blissfully curving her body against his and soaking up its warmth and security.

'I wasn't angry...I was terrified that you were going to wake up and walk out on me. Everything you said and did only confirmed what I already knew...that I'd blown everything.'

'I thought *you* were the one who regretted it. You stopped touching me.'

'Because I was terrified that, if I did, I'd betray how I felt. I suppose I should have guessed that you would run away while I was gone. You've no idea what coming home and finding you gone did to me. And then I found your letter.

'You've written the words, Rosy. Now I want to hear them the way I wanted to hear them the night we made love...I want to feel you whispering them against my skin, crying them into the darkness. They'll be the music to which we'll make love, and I promise you I'll make the same music for you.'

Her heart lifted and somersaulted.

'Oh, and by the way,' Callum added more prosaically, 'we've got exactly this one short weekend together on our own. Elliott and Bea will be arriving on Monday, and from then on, until we get married, Elliott informs me that you'll be staying with them.

'You were wrong about one thing, by the way, my love. Elliott never thought you'd fallen for him. He was just concerned about the way you'd been living. He wanted you to go out and meet more people. He thought a brief stay with William would achieve that. He admitted that he was surprised that you agreed to go so readily.

'I suspect that neither William nor Miranda are going to enjoy their next visit home. He had some pretty scathing things to say about them.'

'They only wanted to protect Bea,' Rosy palliated.

'Mm...and now Elliott wants to protect you. The cottage won't be the same without you. I want to marry you, Rosy, as quickly as possible.'

Her face glowed.

'Ah, my love, if only you'd looked at me like that that morning...how different things would have been. That look says you're a woman deeply in love.'

'I didn't think you'd want me to love you.'

'And do you now?' he asked her, holding her hand against the frantic pound of his heart.

'Yes,' she told him simply.

'Mm,' he said huskily when he had finished kissing her. 'We've got two days on our own. How shall we spend them? Planning the wedding, or making love?'

'Why don't we do both?' Rosy responded demurely, looking at him lovingly.

And that was exactly what they did.

Harlequin Presents

Coming Next Month

Available in September wherever paperback books are sold, or through Harlequin Reader Service:

In the U.S.
901 Fuhrmann Blvd.
P.O. Box 1397
Buffalo, N.Y. 14240-1397

In Canada
P.O. Box 603
Fort Erie, Ontario
L2A 5X3

HARLEQUIN
American Romance

THE LOVES OF A CENTURY...

Join American Romance in a nostalgic look back at the Twentieth Century—at the lives and loves of American men and women from the turn-of-the-century to the dawn of the year 2000.

Journey through the decades from the dance halls of the 1900s to the discos of the seventies ... from Glenn Miller to the Beatles ... from Valentino to Newman ... from corset to miniskirt ... from beau to Significant Other.

Relive the moments ... recapture the memories.

Look now for the CENTURY OF AMERICAN ROMANCE series in Harlequin American Romance. In one of the four American Romance titles appearing each month, for the next twelve months, we'll take you back to a decade of the Twentieth Century, where you'll relive the years and rekindle the romance of days gone by.

Don't miss a day of the CENTURY OF AMERICAN ROMANCE.

A CENTURY OF
AMERICAN ROMANCE
1900's

The women...the men...the passions...
the memories....

Harlequin Superromance®

THE LIVING WEST

Where men and women must be strong in both body and spirit; where the lessons of the past must be fully absorbed before the present can be understood; where the dramas of everyday lives are played out against a panoramic setting of sun, red earth, mountain and endless sky....

Harlequin Superromance is proud to present this powerful new trilogy by Suzanne Ellison, a veteran Superromance writer who has long possessed a passion for the West. Meet Joe Henderson, whose past haunts him—and his romance with Mandy Larkin; Tess Hamilton, who isn't sure she can make a life with modern-day pioneer Brady Trent, though she loves him desperately; and Clay Gann, who thinks the cultured Roberta Wheeler isn't quite woman enough to make it in the rugged West....

Please join us for HEART OF THE WEST (September 1990), SOUL OF THE WEST (October 1990) and SPIRIT OF THE WEST (November 1990) and see the West come alive!

SR-LW-420-1